I AM ALGONQUIN

AN ALGONQUIN QUEST NOVEL

I
AM
ALGONQUIN

Rick Revelle

DUNDURN
TORONTO

Editor: Jennifer McKnight
Design: Jesse Hooper
Printer: Webcom

Library and Archives Canada Cataloguing in Publication

Revelle, Rick
    I am Algonquin : an Algonquin quest novel / by Rick Revelle.

Issued also in electronic formats.
ISBN 978-1-4597-0718-4

    1. Algonquin Indians--Juvenile fiction. I. Title.

PS8635.E887I26 2013   jC813'.6   C2013-900811-X

1   2   3   4   5   17 16 15 14 13

Conseil des Arts du Canada   Canada Council for the Arts   Canadă   ONTARIO ARTS COUNCIL   CONSEIL DES ARTS DE L'ONTARIO

We acknowledge the support of the **Canada Council for the Arts** and the **Ontario Arts Council** for our publishing program. We also acknowledge the financial support of the **Government of Canada** through the **Canada Book Fund** and **Livres Canada Books**, and the **Government of Ontario** through the **Ontario Book Publishing Tax Credit** and the **Ontario Media Development Corporation**.

Care has been taken to trace the ownership of copyright material used in this book. The author and the publisher welcome any information enabling them to rectify any references or credits in subsequent editions.

J. Kirk Howard, President

The publisher is not responsible for websites or their content unless they are owned by the publisher.

Printed and bound in Canada.

VISIT US AT
Dundurn.com | @dundurnpress | Facebook.com/dundurnpress | Pinterest.com/dundurnpress

Dundurn	Gazelle Book Services Limited	Dundurn
3 Church Street, Suite 500	White Cross Mills	2250 Military Road
Toronto, Ontario, Canada	High Town, Lancaster, England	Tonawanda, NY
M5E 1M2	L41 4XS	U.S.A. 14150

In memory of my grandfather,
Mordy Cota, and Alex Aitchison

AUTHOR'S NOTE

Some time ago a person asked me how long I've been an Indian. My answer was since the day I was born.

Out of ignorance and lack of information a lot of people have no idea about who we are as Natives.

We cannot be lumped into one linguistic or cultural group. We have been and still are a collection of Nations in a Nation called Turtle Island.

We weren't discovered; we were here long before anyone thought of looking.

European people said that they were created in Europe, but when we say that we were created on Turtle Island, they point out "oh no, you crossed the Bering Strait." (Quoted from Dan the Lakota Elder in *Neither Wolf Nor Dog* by Kent Nerburn.) What right do they have telling us this?

Ever since I was a young boy I had a story in my head waiting to get out. I knew very little about my ancestors. What I did know was that my Great, Great, Great Grandfather Oliver Cota in the 1840s brought his family from the Petite Nations, an Algonquin reserve in Quebec, and built a log cabin in Bedford Township north of Kingston, Ontario. The cabin still stands to this day.

However, what of before — before the Europeans stumbled across Turtle Island? Who were we, how did we survive and live in this land?

The story you are about to read is a book of fiction, but it is as historically accurate as possible. It is the story of the Omàmiwinini (Algonquin People) in the early 1300s and how they lived.

There is very little written about the Algonquins and artifacts are few and far between. I travelled from Thunder Bay to Newfoundland and points in between to do my research. The Internet proved to be an immense help, but again there is very little information written about my ancestral Nation. What exists is informative and historically important. As difficult as it was to gather information, I gleaned bits and pieces from many sources and interwove it into my story. Museums in Thunder Bay, Midland, Ottawa, Quebec City, and St. John's, Newfoundland, helped to give me the insight I needed. These museums were able to aid me with small tidbits of information about my people that I was able to use. Again the recurring theme repeated itself, very little information about the Algonquins. In the two years of writing my story, I read twelve books that were able to shed some light on my people, how they lived, warred, and interacted with themselves, their allies, and enemies. None of these books, though, were a definitive story of my people.

My most important acquisition was an Algonquin dictionary for which I am deeply indebted to David Bate of the Ardoch Algonquin First Nation and Allies for finding and relaying this important document. This document is called *Algonquin Lexicon* by Ernest McGregor for the Kitigan Zibi Education Council.

In the end, my research was a long, drawn-out affair that came together like a jigsaw puzzle.

As you read this novel the two hopes that I have are that you learn something that you didn't know about the Algonquins and their Allies, and that it will help in a small way to bring attention to the Algonquin language.

I want to give special thanks to Max Finklestein for his knowledge of canoeing the Ottawa River watershed. All of my friends at the Colonnade Golf and Country Club, Marie from Queens University, Jim Corrigan, Frank Gommer, and the twins Lauren and Adrie for my character foundations. My new friends at the Glen Lawrence Golf Club for giving me even more future personalities to work with. Larry and Yvonne Porter for believing. My Mohawk golfing buddy and true friend, Ed Maracle. My sisters Vicki Babcock and Cindy Vorstenbosch for their constructive criticisms. My wife Muriel for all her help. My final thanks to my wonderful friend who meticulously edited my book, Janette St Brock.

This book was made possible through a grant from the Canada Arts Council Aboriginal Emerging Writers Program.

My name is Mahingan, which means wolf in my language, and I am Omàmiwinini (Algonquin) from the Kitcisìpiriniwak tribe (People of the Great River), one of the eight Algonquin tribes of the Ottawa Valley.

I was born right after the warming period that my ancestors had lived through, mild winters, and warm summers. When I was birthed, it was the start of the great cooling period of colder winters and cooler summers. I was born in the year 1305, and this is my story … the story of an Algonquin warrior and a forefather of the Great Chief Tessouat.

1

THE HUNT

I WOKE UP WITH the stark realization that I was in unrecognizable surroundings. It took me a few seconds to remember where I was and why I was there. My small hunting party and I were six days into a trip north to find game.

We had built a small cedar enclosure for the evening and this is where I awoke. The shelter was made entirely of cedar boughs and small saplings used to hold the boughs in place. With five warriors, two young boys, and three animosh (dogs), the body heat and small fire kept us very warm. We had built five of these along the way and some would serve us on the return trip for shelter.

The winter was starting out to be one of hunger for the Omàmiwinini. Very little snow made the hunting of the mònz (moose) and wàwàshkeshi (deer) difficult for us. Without deep snow to slow the animals down and tire them out, we were having a gruelling time trying to hunt them with our lances and arrows.

The decision had been made among five family units that we would each provide a hunter to go in the direction of Kaibonokka (God of the North Wind) and the Land of the Nippissing to find game. There the snow would be deeper and the game would not escape us as readily.

In the summer, all the Algonquin family units come together and hunt, fish, collect berries, nuts, and fruit, and live as a large village. This is to provide protection against our enemies, who find it easier in the summer to raid, and it gives us a chance to trade and plan for the future.

In the winter we must split into the smaller family units because many of the animals have gone to sleep in their dens and the ice covers the lakes and streams, making the fish hard to get to. With the smaller family units we ensure that we won't over-hunt an area, whereas a larger village would decimate the game in no time. This winter, though, the snows were late and my people were starting to feel hunger pangs. A scarce diet of adjidamò (squirrel) and wàbòz (rabbit) did not keep the hunger at bay for long. If we had to eat our berries and other reserves without the meat we needed, starvation would not be far behind. After waking we started on our way. It was very cold and the sundogs were warning us of colder weather. We could hear the loud cracking of the trees in the forest as the frost started to do its work.

With my fur hat, heavy mitts, fur robes, and moccasins, I was starting to work up a sweat with our quick pace. However, my face could feel the sharpness of

Kaibonokka's breath and I would soon have to put a scarf of adjidamò across my face.

My companions were all bundled up like myself, and we carried our lances in our hands, using them for support in the rough terrain. Our bows were slung over our backs with our arrow quivers, as well as our àgimag (snowshoes) that we used for the deep snow. Our knives and clubs were tucked into our leather belts.

My two brothers, Kàg (Porcupine) and Wàgosh (Fox), were with me. Kàg was a fierce warrior and had a dent in his head from a Haudenosaunee (Iroquois) war club many years ago. The wound had long since healed, but he still suffered at times from unexplained head pain. My other brother was younger than Kàg and me. Wàgosh was a good tracker and hunter, but he had yet to be tested in battle.

The other two hunters were married to our sisters. Mònz (Moose) was a large man who carried three lances and no arrows. Mònz lost his two fingers on his right hand next to his thumb in battle with the Nippissing. Without these fingers Mònz could not draw a bowstring, but he was very expert with the lance in war and hunting.

The last hunter, Makwa (Bear), always walked as the rear guard of our column and was forever vigilant. Makwa was not from our tribe, the River People; he was Sàgaiganininiwak (People of the Lake). Makwa was the eldest and a veteran warrior and hunter.

Also with us were Kàg's twin sons who were close to leaving their childhood and had not yet been given a warrior's name. They were Agwingos (Chipmunk) and Esiban (Raccoon). Agwingos and Esiban were responsible for collecting firewood, tending the fire, looking after the dogs, and learning all they could. The dogs were brought along to help run down any game we found, to guard the camp, and also to help carry what we killed back on a travois when we had enough for our needs. As a last resort the dogs were also used for food if our hunt turned out to be unsuccessful.

On our sixth day of walking, we came upon a deer that had fallen through the ice along the shore of a small lake, enabling us to slay it without much effort. Our hope was Nokomis (Earth Mother) would supply us with more than this small doe. After thanking Nokomis for the deer, we dressed it and hung it in a large tree out of sight. We were starting to get nervous as we travelled farther north, because at the best of times the Nippissing people were not tolerant of anyone hunting in their lands.

The day was getting colder and the snow was getting deeper. This cheered us up. With deep snow our chances of finding and killing any large game increased greatly. We were now wearing our àgimag and making good time. We had been keeping to the woods along a small river, partly for concealment and also to stay out of the biting wind. When the sun was high we stopped to eat. Agwingos and Esiban had a fire going and we roasted on sticks some of the deer that we had earlier killed. Melting snow on a piece of bark held above the fire gave us water to drink, and we were soon on our way again.

Soon after our departure the dogs got a scent of something and Wàgosh found fresh signs of a big ayàbe mònz (bull moose). This large animal would sustain our families for a long time.

We picked up our pace and the dogs were running and howling with the excitement of the hunt. Agwingos and Esiban were straining to keep up with us, and we soon came out into a clearing where fires years ago had destroyed the trees. There we saw that the moose was struggling to get through the entanglement of downed trees and deep snow. The large miskoz-i animosh (red dog) had him by the rear leg and the moose kicked him off a couple of times before the other two dogs reached the prey. Both went for the moose's head. The smallest of the three was clamped onto the nostrils and the bull was violently shaking his head and bellowing, trying to disengage him. The more the moose shook, the deeper the pìsà animosh (small dog) clamped onto the nostrils. The small dog was covered with blood and froth from the bull. The wàbàndagawe animosh (white dog) had been caught by the large antlers and was thrown about twenty-five feet by the massive neck strength of the animal. As she hit the ground, a large gush of air could be heard leaving her body, accompanied by a shrill yelp. The dog was up immediately, rushed the bull, and clamped onto the large neck with a renewed viciousness. The snow around the big bull and dogs was red with blood from the four animals. The sound of the dogs barking and the moose's bellowing brought bumps to my skin. There was nothing like the thrill of a hunt to make me feel like my blood had been given a sudden rush through my body.

Mònz was running ahead of the rest of us toward the death struggle of the dogs and moose. In quick succession he hurled two of his lances into the back of the bull. We loosed our arrows and the big moose started to falter. With the dogs upon him, two lances and ten arrows into him, he was on his knees. He was still bellowing and fighting off the dogs, but his lifeblood was slowly leaving him. By now we had drawn our clubs; avoiding his huge swinging antlers, we started hitting him on the head, crushing his skull.

Within minutes the huge animal let out a sudden rush of air from his lungs, causing blood to run from both his nostrils and mouth. This was his final act. We all thanked Nokomis for this gift to her children and started cutting. The warmth of the bull's insides after we had started to butcher him helped keep our hands warm. The dogs were rewarded with the intestines and Mònz was given the heart, as he was the first to strike. Kàg and I worked on cutting around the head and legs to peel off the hide. Agwingos and Esiban were given the job of removing the lances and arrows from the carcass. They also had the job of cutting the horns off, which would be used to make fish hooks, arrow and lance heads, and other weapons. The women would also make utensils out of the huge rack. Our people would use every piece of meat, bone, and hide that we could carry back from this giant of the forest.

Wàgosh and Makwa had gone back into the woods to cut small trees down so we could make pimidàbà-jigan (travois) for the dogs and odàbànàks (toboggans) to transport the moose back to our village. We used pieces of his hide to hold the meat on the travois. With the extra weight of the bull and the doe, our return trip home would take three days longer.

Sound carries a long distance in the wintertime, and I was wary that the echoes of this kill would bring unwanted attention from any Nippissing in the area. As these thoughts went through my mind, the small dog stuck his head into the air and I could see his nostrils flare. Then he started to growl. Looking in the direction that he was pointed, I realized my worst fear.

2

THE ENCOUNTER

IN THE DISTANCE, ALONG the tree line, I picked up some sudden movements. We were hunting in the Nippissing territory and any intrusion would not bode kindly with them. The Haudenosaunee had been raiding their villages lately, and they would defend their hunting grounds with blood against all intruders.

With the growing length of the winter, food would also be at a premium with the Nippissing. They would want this moose for their families just as much as we wanted it for ours. The huge animal affected more than just the Nippissing and Omàmiwinini hunters' lives. Without the life-sustaining meat, starvation would not be far behind for either tribe's families. This dead beast could both prevent, but also cause, more death in the future.

With Wàgosh and Mònz cutting poles in the woods along our back trail, they would have no way of knowing that we were about to be set upon. They were probably at least ten or more minutes away. We would need them and quickly. I motioned to Agwingos and Esiban to come toward me, without causing any suspicion to the hunters who were silently coming upon us. I asked the twins to take the red dog and to find Wàgosh and Mònz's trail and bring them back as quickly as possible. They were to tell them that we were in danger. I instructed the boys that when they left they were not to run until they reached the cover of the tree line. This was so they would not draw attention to the fact that they were any more than a couple of young boys shirking their duties and going off on a walk.

As soon as the boys left, I told Kàg and Makwa what I had observed and what my suspicions were. We decided that we would continue with the butchering, not letting our adversaries know that we had spotted them. It would take the boys at least ten or fifteen minutes to get to where our companions were. They would not be able to get back to assist us for at least twenty minutes to half an hour, so Kàg, Mònz, and I had to be prepared. While working, we took turns watching the progress of the enemy. They had stayed inside the tree line to the west of us. As we continued with our task, each of us slowly took our arrows out of our quivers and stuck them in the snow beside us, enabling easier access to the weapons. The Nippissing were working their way to an area that would leave them with only about fifty feet of open ground between us. They most likely assumed that we hadn't seen them. This would give them a distinct advantage in surprising us as they could cover the ground before we could be ready ourselves. We still did not know how many there were, but we estimated at least four or five by the shadowy sightings.

We had planned it so the moose carcass would be between us and our attackers for cover. I glanced up and witnessed the first man run out of the woods. Quickly grabbing my bow, I loosed an arrow. The impact of the missile hitting the man in the hip could be heard in the cold silence. With a shrill yell he dropped down, reddening the snow around him. Immediately, two arrows hit the moose near where I was crouching with distinctive thuds. Makwa and Kàg had also gotten off arrows; Kàg's entered the throat of a young hunter. The man could not scream but just knelt in the snow trying to pull the arrow out of his neck. This made the wound larger and allowed the blood to spurt with every beat of his heart.

In an instant they were on us like a pack of wolves, screaming and yelling. There were five more besides the two we had hit with our arrows. Makwa had been the closest to them as they reached us and three of them were trying to take the huge man down. Makwa was a big man and I only came to his shoulders in height. His bravery in battle was legendary, but if neither Kàg nor I could get to him the Nippissing would overpower him by sheer numbers.

The two remaining dogs, sensing that Makwa was in immediate danger, rushed the warrior nearest to them and dragged him down by burying their canine fangs into the man's thighs. The dogs were snapping and growling like wolves and their prey was screaming and lashing out at them with a huge war club and knife.

Kàg and one of the Nippissing were swinging wildly at each other with their clubs, hitting glancing blows off each other. As I made my way toward Makwa, I encountered the last warrior that was between me and the main body of snarling dogs and screaming men. I could see the fear in my foe's eyes as he ran toward me. He, like the rest of his party, were all young and probably had been battle tested against the Haudenosaunee in the last couple of years.

My first instinct was to try and kneecap him with my club. If I swung at his head, he would only block it, and I would be wide open for a return strike. I dropped to one knee in the soft snow and swung with all my might at his knees. He was quicker than I had expected and jumped over my swinging club. While he was in the air he twisted and swung his axe and caught me with a glancing blow on the right side of my head, knocking my hat off and lacerating my ear. When the Nippissing landed, he stumbled just enough that I could come down with my war club on the top of his right shoulder. I could feel the bone breaking underneath my weapon. He screamed like a mishi-pijiw (panther) and switched his axe to the other hand and swung again at me as I was closing in. I blocked his weapon with my left forearm and could feel a tingling in my wrist as I took the brunt of the force of the axe's shaft. With a mighty scream, I swung my club and caught the young warrior full in the face. The man dropped and lay motionless at my feet.

I then turned my attention toward the sound of the dogs and Makwa. The animals had torn the pants completely off of their adversary. The man was fighting for his life and had cut the small dog on its withers with his bone knife. Men and animals were covered with blood, as was the snow around them. The beleaguered warrior finally broke free and ran back from where he had come.

Meanwhile, Makwa was in distress. He had a knife embedded in his shoulder and blood running down his face from a head wound. He was valiantly trying to fend off his attackers, but they had gotten the upper hand on him. Both of his attackers were bloodied. However, one had worked his way around Makwa and with all his might swung down on Makwa's head with a large club made out of a huge tree knot. Makwa dropped to his knees and just as the Nippissing was swinging again, there was a blood-curdling scream as a massive spear tore into the back of the man. Without a sound, the remaining warrior took one look at Mònz and Wàgosh running toward the battle, and ran off with the speed of a frightened deer. The battle between Kàg and his foe ended with the entrance of Wàgosh and Mònz. Kàg's adversary broke off the encounter and ran.

The three fleeing Nippissing grabbed the dead man with the arrow in his throat and also the warrior with the arrow in his thigh. They escaped to the tree line. I turned to look at the man I had battled with and all that remained was a pool of blood. I could see him in the distance staggering toward the tree line following the remnants of the group.

We didn't disturb the body of the dead man that they left behind. We would leave him where he had fallen and his fellow warriors would come back for his body. Our group did not give chase, as these men had suffered enough, and we had to make our escape from their lands. Two of them had died and two were badly wounded, and the latter might not survive unless they could get them to their healer.

For us, we had suffered a huge loss. Makwa, my sister's man, had fallen in battle. There would be great sorrow when we arrived back at our village with this news. With a journey home longer than the six days we took to get here, we would have to bury Makwa on the trail.

Neither Kàg nor his foe had suffered any wounds, but my ear was still bleeding from the axe blow. I put some willow pumice on it to keep out the poison and some jimsonweed to cover the wound and help it heal.

With not knowing how far the Nippissing had come from their winter homes, we were at a loss as to how long a time frame we had to finish our butchering. Our main fear was that they would return with a larger force and catch us here.

Having this in mind, we had to rush our job at hand. I had the twins tend to the wounded small dog using only willow to mend the injury. If we put jimson-weed on the wound, he would lick it and die from the poison of the herb. We would have to pull a toboggan with Makwa on it until we could bury him. The twins would have to take on extra duties now that we were short one warrior.

I told the boys that after they tended to the dogs they were to start a fire and roast some moose for us. I calculated that we had to get the big bull butchered, make the travois and toboggans, and be away from there by morning light. We would use mònzwegin (moose hide) and some woody vines to make binding for the carriers. Time was of the essence.

The farther away we got from this battle site the less stomach the Nippissing would have to follow us. But we knew they would not forget this intrusion and the losses they had suffered.

3

THE BURIAL

WITH A LARGE FIRE snapping away, we proceeded to make the five toboggans that were needed for the trip back to our villages. Each of the four hunters had to pull a toboggan, plus the twins had to take turns with the other. The red dog and the white one pulled a travois. The small dog was not required to because of its wound. The travois poles were easy to strap on the dogs. Using moose hide, we fastened it across the two poles and then the load was tied down.

The twins now, besides tending the fire and cooking us some meat, also had to cut leather strips from the moose hide for the bindings, plus cut us lengths of the wild grape vines for added strength. The dogs were our sentries that night, as every one else had a job to do. They had been fed well, and even though they were content with full bellies, they were alert.

Kàg and I heated the green poles that had been cut for the toboggans in the fire. The poles had to be heated so one end could be bent without breaking. The front end of the sleds had to have an upward curve on them so they could be pulled without digging into the snow. Once they were heated enough and bent, Wàgosh and Mònz tied the poles with leather bindings and sat the framework that they had built on top. The leather was laid in small grooves to keep from interfering with the pulling of the toboggan. The poles were then kept as tightly together as possible to avoid gaps that the snow could come through. Leather pieces of the hide were then tied from the framework to the curved section to keep the bent poles from springing back out of shape. With all of us working together we had the toboggans and travois ready well before daylight. Everyone then ate and we hurriedly erected a small lean-to with the remaining poles facing the fire. After covering it with cedar boughs, we slept through the rest of the cold night.

With the approach of dawn we loaded all the toboggans with the moose meat and the body of Makwa. We took all that we could load on the sleds and left the rest. If the Nippissing came back this way before any wolves arrived, they would find enough meat to feed themselves for a while. We all had the burden of extra weight until the time came that we could bury Makwa. Agwingos and the small dog led us. Following them was Esiban pulling a toboggan. The twins would take turns pulling the sled whenever one or the other tired, and then the other twin had to lead us on the trail we had travelled here on. Plus be a lookout. Wàgosh, Kàg,

Mònz, and I followed in that order. I pulled the sled with
the body of Makwa plus as much meat as I could carry.
The other two dogs brought up the rear; they needed
packed down snow to pull their travois. The red dog
had the antlers and a bit of meat and the white dog had
the large hide. We had tied pieces of hide around all the
dogs' feet to protect their pads and to keep snow from
collecting between their toes.

The start of the day was bitterly cold and our breath
hung like clouds in the air. The only sounds that could
be heard at the outset were the breaking of the snow
under our moccasins and the creak of the sleds. Even
the twins were too encumbered in their tasks at hand to
be talking and teasing each other. We trudged through
the snow until the sun was high in the sky. Then we
stopped for a meal. The twins untied the red and white
dogs from their travois and started a fire. I asked
Wàgosh to walk ahead for a while to see if all was clear,
and I backtracked for a distance to make sure no one
was on our trail.

In half an hour we had a good fire going and meat
cooking. Neither Wàgosh nor I had seen any activity
in either direction. Kàg mentioned though that he had
noticed a wind change and that Kaibonokka's brother
Shawano (God of the South Wind) was starting to blow.
That meant that a storm was approaching, and we might
have to sit it out as soon as we found good shelter. Mònz
reminded us of the rock overhang that we had passed
previously on our journey. If we could make it there
before the storm hit, there would be adequate cover and
we could sit out the tempest that was coming our way.

The only advantage about the approaching storm was that it would make the Nippissing think twice about following us if they had thoughts of revenge.

After we had finished our meals, we melted enough snow to fill our small clay water casks that we all carried around our waists. Everyone then took their place in line and we continued on our journey. With the shifting wind and the snow starting to sting our faces, we were in for an uncomfortable trek. With bent heads we struggled against the cold and the snow, everyone straining against the leather ropes that pulled their toboggans. The only thing that kept us going was the realization that we would reach a sheltered area and be able to rest, eat, and feel safe in a haven protected from the elements that would want to harm us. We prayed to Kitchi Manitou (Father of Life) to guide us to the rock overhang.

Finally, after what felt like an eternity, Esiban, with the small dog in tow, ran down the line saying that he could see through the snow to the area where the outcrop was. Within minutes we were sheltered. The rock had an overhang that enabled us to go back into a small cliff about twenty feet; the roof itself was about twelve feet high. The floor of the small cave was dirt, and we easily built a fire. Some of the smoke escaped out from under the rock, but what stayed stung our eyes. This was no different than being in our lodges. We always had problems with our smouldering fires burning our eyes and causing them to water, because as hard as we tried, we couldn't get the smoke to dissipate. Some of our people, as they grew older developed eye problems from the cooking and heating fires in their lodges.

Outside the cave we were well guarded by tall cedar, pine, and a couple of dirt mounds. Agwingos and Esiban collected wood, and we put the loaded sleds at the back of the cave so the meat would stay frozen. Kàg made a large spit and hung a good portion of moose meat over the fire. Wàgosh and I took the body of Makwa and put him well away from the fire. Our hope was that the fire would thaw the ground enough for us to bury this great warrior as close to his final battle as we could.

After we ate and drank, Mònz started telling stories. During this time I took some charcoal from the fire and some bloodroot I had in my satchel. With my paints I went to the rock wall closest to the flickering fire and started to draw the story of the hunt of the moose and the battle that ensued. Whoever came this way would know that brave men had battled and died so that their families would not starve. After I finished my drawings, I sat down for the first watch and looked over the small band of Omàmiwinini that I was leading. There was Kàg, my oldest brother and the father of Agwingos and Esiban. Kàg was a head taller than me but lighter in weight. He always wore two hawk feathers in his hair and had an earring of a bear claw in one ear. On his forehead, where he had the dent from the Haudenosaunee war club, he had drawn a tattoo of the sun to keep the spot warm because his headaches felt like ice.

Wàgosh, our younger brother, was just entering warrior-hood. No longer a young boy, Wàgosh had undergone the Wysoccan Journey and had left his childhood behind. Wàgosh was taller than Kàg, heavily muscled, and always wore a foxtail in his hair. He had a large scar on his cheek that he received during a summer trading session with the Malecite. It was the result of a lacrosse game that all the young boys of the two tribes had been playing. The game had become rough and bloody. His prize possession was a knife he had made out of the horn of his first hunt, a large white-tailed nàbe (buck).

Mònz, our brother-in-law, was a warrior and great hunter. The loss of two fingers in a battle with the Nippissing years before had forced him to become expert with the lance. He was a huge man and in battle or the hunt he was always the first to strike. He wore a necklace of bear claws of a nòjek (female bear) that did not take kindly of him stumbling on her and her makòns (cubs) one spring past. In the ensuing battle Mònz struck a fatal blow with his knife to the bear's throat, but Mònz wore the scars of the combat. His left shoulder had deep scars from the claw of the bear, plus along the left side of his neck her mark was also prominent. If he hadn't been with a hunting party that day he would have died in the woods. It took many weeks and the intense healing power of our Shaman to save his life. Learning the lesson from the bear, now it is Mònz who always strikes first.

For my part, I am known as Mahingan because my eyes have the slant of the gray wolf. I have seen twenty-five or more summers and have led my tribe since the passing of my father. The Shaman had told my father before he died that I would be great leader. In my hair I wear three misise (turkey) feathers because the wild turkey is one of the bravest animals in the forest. In my ears are the claws of a wolf, and now I have only part of the top of my right ear because of the Nippissing war axe.

The twins Agwingos and Esiban still have a few years to live until they have to take the Wysoccan Journey. They are active, always do what they are told, and are a great help whenever we take them hunting. The dogs stay with the boys at all times because they always make a fuss over them and are responsible for their feeding. Their looks are very similar, and at times they are hard to tell apart. In the winter we make Esiban wear his namesake's fur as a hat. That way we can recognize them. In the summer it is anyone's guess telling them apart.

The three dogs that we had with us were great hunters and war dogs. The huge red male dog and the white female dog were mates. The small dog was one of their pups, but he never grew as big as his parents did. His problem was he never backed down from a fight and was covered with scars along with his new wound from the Nippissing knife. Dogs are an important companion for the Omàmiwinini because they serve many purposes for us: beasts of burden, hunters, camp guards, and food in times of near starvation.

Feeling my eyes grow heavy, I woke Wàgosh for the next watch. Before I went to sleep, I walked out of the cave to relieve myself and to check on the weather. The snow was still coming down heavily and the wind was making the flakes dance in the air like the leaves on a windy day in autumn. We would be here one more day, at least until we could bury Makwa and leave. The snowfall did serve one good purpose: it kept the

Nippissing off our trail. I went back toward the fire and lay near the dogs and the twins and fell asleep at once.

The next day we spent reinforcing our sleds and checking our snowshoes, making necessary repairs and adjustments. The twins kept the fire going and played outside with the dogs. Agwingos and Esiban were also given the job of making more leather moccasins for the dogs. They had unloaded one toboggan and made good use of a small hill for play. Every time they rode the sled to the bottom of the hill the dogs ran along the side, barking. Standing to watch for a while I couldn't figure out who was having more fun, the dogs or the twins. When the boys pulled the toboggan back up the hill on the run, the dogs nipped at their heels. This group would definitely sleep soundly tonight. As soon as the sun was high, I backtracked on our trail for a time and Mònz did the same on our intended trail ahead. Nothing was sighted and with the storm almost blown out, we would be heading out the next day. Before we left, we would bury Makwa where the fire was and cover the area so it wouldn't look disturbed.

That next morning the six of us were able to dig deep enough to bury Makwa. Each of us cut a lock of his hair for our medicine pouch, and we thanked Kitchi Manitou for his past life and offered prayers to help him on his way to the afterlife. We lit a pipe and blew smoke to the four brother winds, Kaibonokka, Kabun (West), Shawano, and Wabun (East). After singing a death song, we left with deep sorrow in our hearts for the loss of such a great hunter, warrior, and friend. However, happiness would soon replace our sadness because we knew that Kitchi Manitou would lead him to the Spirit World.

Without our snowshoes we would have been up over our knees in snow. The pulling of the sleds was heavy work, putting a strain on us all, but we were in good spirits knowing that this food would keep our families nourished for many days. The twins switched back and forth, pulling their sled, and led the column with the small dog. Sometimes though, his weight was too much for the crust of the snow, and he fell in up to his neck. But he struggled on. Wàgosh, Kàg, Mònz, and I switched spots in line every so often; that way one person wasn't always having the hard pulling.

To hasten our time, that day we ate while we walked. We had been gone nine days and there had been very little food in the village when we had left. It was still bitterly cold, but I was sweating underneath all my layers of fur. The areas not covered by our scarves were at risk from the wind. We rubbed moose fat on the exposed skin to keep the elements from freezing the bare spots. Looking around at my companions, I saw the strain in their faces and the steam billowing from their bodies. Breath came out of our mouths like the puffs of smoke from a smouldering fire. The two dogs were always bringing up the rear because the walking was easier for the travois that they pulled. As I looked back at the dogs I sensed nervousness in the pair, and they were looking back sniffing the air. The wind had changed from the south since the storm. Now it was again at our back from the north. Seeing the nervousness of the dogs, I told everyone to get closer to the thicker forest and take a rest. There was also one other sign that I could see in the sky, and it was a warning of what I knew was coming. Three kàgàgi (ravens) were following us. I instructed the twins to not start a fire, but to collect firewood and prepare in case we had to stay. I also told them to tie up the small dog and to not take the travois off the other two. I decided to backtrack on our trail to see what was bothering the dogs. Asking my fellow three hunters to be vigilant, I left my sled with them and cautiously retraced our trail.

Within fifteen minutes I crested a small hill and was able to look off into the distance. There I could see what alarmed the dogs. There were ten mahingans following the leader who had them on a steady lope on our trail. The ravens were never wrong, and there was the proof in front of me. We would not be able to run from them. Standing and fighting would have to be the order of that day. I bent down and took my snowshoes off. I would need to run as fast as I could to get back to the group. Again we would have to fight to keep this moose. The survival of our families depended on what was going to take place in the next hour or so.

4

DEATH IN THE SNOW

GASPING FOR AIR WHEN I reached my hunting party, I instructed Wàgosh to start a fire. Agwingos and Esiban were asked to tie the three dogs to the trees about twenty feet behind the fire. I further advised them to take the fur hides off of the dogs' feet to make them battle-ready and to have their knives prepared to cut the dogs free if they were threatened.

Kàg asked what the danger was.

"Kàg, what does the Raven usually bring with him when there is meat or carrion about?"

"Your namesake: Wolf! How many are there?"

"I counted ten, plus the pack leader," I said.

I then started shouting out orders and outlined our defence. I told my small group, "We have maybe fifteen minutes before they arrive. They are hungry and want the moose meat. We must be prepared with a defence, because they will circle us looking for a weak spot. We cannot let the dogs loose unless it is absolutely necessary; the size of this pack would tear them to shreds. Mònz, because you cannot shoot a bow, you will have to be behind us guarding the meat and the twins. I will face the trail where the leader and his mate will come. Kàg, you must defend the left and Wàgosh the right. We have to hope and pray our arrows fly true to the mark, because these animals are hungry and determined."

It would be dark in a short time and the wolves would strike in the dim light. The sun was falling near the treetops, lighting the snow and the approaching beasts in a fiery red hue. They started to howl, sending a chill through my body. With this as a signal they broke into a run. Our dogs then started barking. Hearing this, the attackers immediately stopped and began snarling. The male and female pair jumped to the front and snapped in our direction. They were still a good distance away, but I loosed an arrow that flew toward the female. She moved at the last second and the arrow struck a young wolf in the chest with a resounding thump. The pack, sensing danger, pulled back as the younger wolf howled in pain.

The pack now sat as if waiting for instructions. Then they all started running in different directions. Wàgosh let out a warning and Kàg turned just in time to see two large wolves running toward him. He had no time to string his bow, so he grabbed his lance from the snow. At that instance another lance flew through the air and embedded itself in the lead wolf's neck. Without a sound the animal dropped. The ever-wary Mònz had struck again. Kàg dropped to one knee as the other wolf sprung toward him. His lance caught the attacker full in the chest. Kàg was covered with the animal's blood as both tumbled into the snow.

Then, upon hearing our dogs snarling and Esiban screaming, I looked around and saw Agwingos on the back of a large wolf that had his brother pinned face down in the snow. Agwingos was stabbing the wolf while Mònz was running to the aid of the boys. On the way past the dogs he cut off their leather ties with a slash of his spear blade. The dogs beat Mònz to the struggling twins and the wolf. First in battle was the small dog, and he lunged at the face of the wolf. The twins were screaming. The wolf was snarling and our dogs were barking. It sounded like a world gone mad. In a matter of seconds the small battle was over. By the time Mònz reached the melee our dogs and Agwingos's knife had finished the intruder.

I turned my eyes back to the remainder of the pack. The female and male leaders of the group had stopped short of our circle. With four of the pack dead and dying, they realized that we were too formidable a prey to defeat. Any more losses to their family and they would have difficulty surviving and defending their territory against other wolf packs. With one last wail at us, they departed the way they had come.

With the retreat of the wolves, we gathered ourselves. Esiban suffered no wounds. This could be attributed to the quick reaction of his brother, the amount of clothes he was wearing, and the efforts of our dogs. We now had four wolf pelts. Because of the bravery of Agwingos and Esiban, they would each receive a pelt to do with as they desired.

We made camp for the evening and built the fire. That night marked the tenth day we had been gone, and we still had at least five or six more days of travel left. The extra load of pulling the meat on the toboggans was delaying our return. The next day we would push harder and try to reach one of our cedar enclosures that we had built on our trip north. We still had to pick up the deer that we had been hanging in a tree along our back trail. Again we would leave a place with the snow covered in blood. We hoped that the rest of our return trip would be uneventful and that Kitchi Manitou would watch over us and lead us in safety.

The fire was high and we ate moose and talked about what was ahead. Kàg took the first watch while the rest of us slept. The dogs didn't need to be tied, as the wolf pack had left this area behind and would not bother us again.

5

THE LONG WALK

NO ONE HAD WAKENED me to take a watch, and I awoke in the faint light of the dawn. I was concerned that something had happened. I noticed Wàgosh sitting with his back to the fire and on watch.

"Brother, why didn't you wake me for my watch?"

Wàgosh answered, "All was fine, and we had decided to split the sentry duties just three ways tonight. We thought that you needed the rest and maybe from this day forward we could let one of us sleep throughout the whole night."

I had made the decision we would have a good first meal of the day, and I added an extra treat. I fashioned a bowl out of birch bark from a fallen tree that I had found. With a sharp small bone, I made a hole in the bark and pulled through the leather strips that I had in my medicine bag. I was then able to sew the bark together, and using pine sap that I had thawed I sealed the bowl. Then I melted snow in it. Next I cut some cedar leaves and put them in the melted water. Tying the vessel above the fire I let it come to a boil. During this time I made some birch bark ladles that we all could dip in the container and with which we could drink our cedar drink. The cedar tea would invigorate us and keep our bodies healthy. Upon seeing what I was doing, everyone's spirits rose. The twins fed the dogs and then hooked the two bigger dogs up to their travois. Then they tied their wolf pelts onto it. Wàgosh, Kàg, and Mònz readied the other sleds and fastened the remaining two pelts onto the toboggans. We then drank our tea and ate. We broke camp and headed toward our homes and families.

As always, the small dog led with the boys following. Kàg, Wàgosh, Mònz, and I fell in behind, with the red and white dogs trailing. The snow was easier to walk on now because in the last few days the temperature had risen, melting the tops of the snow a small bit. Then the temperature fell again making a hard crust strong enough to walk on. We stayed along the trail that had brought us north. The sky was bright blue and cloudless. Everyone was in good spirits and they talked and sang about our accomplishments.

We came upon a stream that connected two small lakes. The area was about one hundred feet wide and completely frozen. The wind had kept the ice clear of snow and the stream ran from our right to left on a gradual grade to the lake below. In the next few minutes we were treated to some comic relief. As the small dog started to run across the frozen stream he slipped and fell. As he tried to get up his legs splayed in four directions and he started to slide down toward the other lake. The twins were roaring with laughter and my fellow warriors also found this turn of events very amusing. The dog now was about halfway toward the lower lake and headed for some open water where a small waterfall produced a strong enough current to keep the water open. I signaled Wàgosh to go to the other side and then both of us tried to get alongside of the dog and catch him before he hit the water. By this time everyone was laughing uproariously. Wàgosh and I reached the dog and stopped him from sliding any further. He was not in the least bit concerned about his ordeal and probably happy to be the centre of attention. Wàgosh took the dog to his side of the stream and Kàg and I held onto the red and white dogs as they crossed. We didn't want two dogs attached to a travois sliding down this icy run. As we continued on our way, the twins were still laughing and talking about the small dog's misadventure.

As we continued, I thought about my wìdigemàgan (wife), Wàbananang (Morning Star). We had been together now for two summers, but there had been no children yet, as the moon had never been right for the seed. She was beautiful and we cared very much for each other. I hoped that she was eating well but inside I knew that food was scarce and the men left behind would have to be cunning and skilled to hunt down any game. I hoped that while we were gone a large snowstorm might have passed through and helped the men in their hunting.

Walking until the sun reached its day's height, we stopped long enough to build a small fire to melt snow for water. After eating the extra food that we had cooked in the morning, we continued on our way. I knew that we were within distance of a cedar shelter that we had erected on our trip up. Hopefully we could make it before too much darkness had set in, but knowing it would be a full moon tonight our band would be able to see the way.

Esiban and the small dog were ahead of us but within sight the rest of the day. The sun had set a long time ago, and we were walking in moonlight. In the light we saw Esiban and the dog running back. He said the shelter was a short distance ahead. Rest would be welcomed tonight.

In short order we reached the cedar enclosure and the twins had a fire going. Mònz had a meal cooking and I was melting snow for water. The dogs were given some frozen meat and all went well.

After we ate, Kàg took out his pipe, tamped in some tobacco, and lit it. We passed it around and thanked Kitchi Manitou for guiding us through the day. We talked about our homes and families and how this meat would sustain their spirits and bodies. Our small group had been gone now ten sunrises, and we were still at least five days from home. Even though our trip north had only taken six days, we had to stay over one day because the snowstorm and the extra loads slowed us down.

"Uncle Mònz," said Agwingos, "can you tell us a story?"

"Yes, please do," said Esiban. "Tell us a tale about one of Nokomis' children."

"Okay," said Mònz. "I will tell you how the wey-nusse (turkey buzzard) got his black feathers.

"When Cluskap (the creator force) made all the animals and pineshìnjish (birds), the Weynusse had bright white feathers and a head like the Kiniw (eagle). Weynusse liked to show off though, and he was always trying to fly higher than all the other birds even higher than the Kiniw. Weynusse said to Cluskap, 'I am the strongest and smartest bird on Turtle Island, much superior to the mighty Kiniw.' Cluskap said to Weynusse, 'Oh vain one, if you brag and show off too much, you will surely become the fool, and it will be your downfall.' Weynusse then said, 'I will show you, Cluskap, that I will be your chosen one to be the Chief of all the skies. I will fly to the sun where no bird has ever gone, and then you will believe me when I say I am the greatest.' With those words Weynusse flew straight to the sun, and as he approached the heat of the big ball, his feathers caught fire and his head became scorched and he turned back to Turtle Island with the scars he carries to this day. His once magnificent head was red and wrinkled and all his feathers were black except for some white ones under his wing that the sun could not reach to burn, and to this day that is all that is left of the Weynusse's magnificent white plumage.

"Never be like the foolish showoff, Weynusse."

With that, Mònz said that he would take the first watch for the night and tend the fire.

The next morning, as I had last watch, I awoke everyone with the rising of the sun and then ate a quick meal and headed toward home. We all knew before we returned to our families that we would have some work to do to prepare for our homecoming.

6

ARRIVING HOME

WE WERE WITHIN A day of our families after being away for a total of fifteen sunrises and everyone was anxious to see their loved ones again. Two days ago we had stopped and picked up the deer that we had left in a tree. It had been a long and arduous trip marked with the deaths of many creatures: moose, deer, wolves, and men. Ours was a hard life, and we always had to be on the ready to kill or be killed. This was what it meant to survive in the harsh surroundings of Turtle Island.

Our muscles were aching from the walk and the loads on the toboggans. The twins were even starting to slow down and talk less. However, with the knowledge that we would soon be home, our spirits lifted. We would eat and prepare ourselves to meet our families after the long trek. There would be stories to tell of battles and death.

Because our group would have to spend one more night on the trail, we needed to build one last cedar shelter. The fire tonight would have to be bright, as we would be shaving the parts of our scalp locks that had grown out on the days we were on the hunt.

We found a good place to camp for our last night. Before long the twins had a big fire going and Wàgosh had a piece of meat on a spit cooking. Kàg was melting snow for water and Mònz was sharpening the clamshells and knives for the job ahead. It was important that our scalps were shaven when we entered the village. Being warriors, our shaved heads were part of this inheritance and also identified us with our band.

We shaved our heads on both sides with a scalp lock in the middle. To make our hair stand up, we layered animal grease on it. All of us had hair that was long at the back and reached down below our shoulders. Into the hair we placed our feathers and animal hair. The twins, not yet being warriors, each had a full head of hair.

It was decided that we would be shaved in order of age, oldest to youngest, so Kàg would go first. With all that they had been through, we decided that the twins could also help in the ritual.

When the water was hot enough, we laid the knives and clamshells into the bark container to warm them. The twins then used some soft hide to wash the part of our heads that were to be shaved. This would soften the bristled hair and make it easier to cut. I then took a knife and started to cut the hair as far down toward the scalp as I could. We used the knives to do the main cutting and the clamshells to finish the close cut. We could sharpen clamshells to a finer edge, thus enabling us to shave close to the scalp. I did most of the cutting and shaving. Usually the women did this, as they had a very steady hand and rarely drew blood. Tonight I was able to shave Kàg, Mònz, and Wàgosh without incident. Kàg returned the favour for me.

After we finished shaving our heads we sang songs to our ancestors and in honour of Makwa. That night we gave the twins another honour. They would take the first watch and tend the fire.

In the morning we had a quick meal and headed on our way. Our absence from the village had been sixteen days. The last few days we had noticed the snow was disappearing and a lot of bare spots were appearing in the open meadows. That was not a good sign for our people that we had left behind. They needed the deep snow to hunt. Unless the hunters that had stayed with our small winter band had any luck at all in securing food, there would be problems. Our small winter band of Kitcisìpiriniwak numbered fifteen men, twenty-one women, and twenty-eight children. With the death of Makwa, we were down to fourteen men. Of the men who were left in the village, four of them had just taken the Wysoccan Journey this past summer and were inexperienced in all aspects of warriorhood. Three of the remaining six were elders, leaving only three men with the stamina and experience to hunt and guard the encampment. Our village consisted of fourteen shelters beside a small stream, sheltered by a large forest of pines and cedars.

After walking for most of the day, we soon came upon the clearing that we knew led to our families and lodges. As we walked into the forest that sheltered our family unit, we were taken aback.

7

HAPPINESS
AND SORROW

OUR SHELTERS WERE OVAL wàginogàns (lodges) made out of birch bark and held together by saplings intertwined on the inside. On the outside we used slabs of cedar to hold the birch bark down, tying them to the frame. The birch bark was overlapped so as not to leak. The saplings on the inside were not tied end to end but were joined side to side to avoid poking holes in the birch bark. The young trees were bent in a curve and fastened together with spruce roots.

What caught us by surprise was that no one was on guard and that we could only see smoke coming out of seven of the wàginogàns.

"Wàgosh, announce our homecoming."

"E-ya-ya-ya-ya," Wàgosh sang. "The hunters have arrived with food and tales of adventure."

Then Wàgosh sang a death song announcing the death of Makwa. With that his wife and our sister

See-Bee-Pee-Nay-Sheese (River Bird) came out of her home, wailing and crying. I took my sister in my arms and told her that Makwa died a warrior's death, and he would enter the afterlife with great honour.

See-Bee-Pee-Nay-Sheese would enter her home and douse her fire. She would mourn face-down on her mat for six days covered by her robes and receive only cold food for nourishment. The families would give her gifts to comfort her. She would not be allowed to marry again until our mother gave her permission.

When an Algonquin warrior marries, he always lived with the wife's family and helped hunt and protect the family unit.

Nijamik (Two Beaver), one of our elders, followed my sister out to the centre of the village leading the rest of the people.

"Mahingan," he said, "we are happy to see you. This food will keep us from starving. We have lost one of the older women and a small child since you have left. Wajashk (Muskrat) took two of the young warriors three days ago to see if they could spear any fish through the open ice of the big river. Hunger has stalked us like an enemy on the warpath. We have huddled together in seven shelters to save wood. The people were getting too weak to forage for wood to burn. Thus the decision was made to come together. Now, though, we see that the Chief and his warriors have returned successfully with meat. Tonight we will feast and hear your stories and how Makwa died. The older women will take turns sitting with See-Bee-Pee-Nay-Sheesh and help her with her mourning. The rest of us will visit her in the days to come and help ease her grief with gifts. The moose and deer will get us through the winter until the bear wakes from his sleep and the elk come to the south from the deep woods. You have saved us, Mahingan. This will be a story for the ages."

When Nijamik finished talking to me, I could feel a hand on mine. I looked around and saw a beautiful smiling face — my wife, Wàbananang. Tonight I would celebrate in many ways.

I followed Wàbananang to our shelter; she had been staying with my mother and her sisters-in-law while I was absent. The lodge was cold from the lack of heat but in a short time we had a fire going. The light from the fire enhanced her striking looks. As we sat and ate she told me what the last days were like with very little food and the people starting to lose heart that our hunt would be successful.

"Mahingan, five nights ago my father came to me in a dream and told me that you and your men had not failed and would be bringing the meat to the village soon. Upon waking, I told everyone my dream, and it raised their hopes. Then you arrived as my father had told me you would. You are a good husband and leader."

"Thank you, my love. Your belief in me strengthens my heart."

With that I led her to where we slept and felt the warmth of her body and the aura that always came over me when we made love. That always was an experience that quenched my soul and gave me the strength to carry on. Making love is a gift from Kitchi Manitou that is one of the great mysteries of being one of his people.

8

SPRING AWAKENING

WE HAD BEEN BACK from our hunt for weeks now and on this day I awoke to the sound of the wind and rain falling on our wàginogàn. Wàbananang was lying at my side, and I could feel the warmth of her body and feel her breath on my neck. I arose without waking her. That day we would start taking the sweet water from the trees in the forest. Everyone helps in the gathering of the onzibàn (sap).

Our women had been busy making the birch bark containers that were used to catch the water. When I left the lodge, I woke Wàbananang and told her I was going out to start notching the trees. She and the other women's job for the coming days would be to tend the fires that heated the sweet water, boiling it in the clay pots that made the sweet thick syrup we enjoyed. The clay pots that our women used for boiling the syrup had been obtained from the Ouendat in trade.

Everyone also liked to drink the tree's water and cook our food in it. This was one of the things that our people looked forward to in the spring, harvesting the sweet water. After a long winter, this was Nokomis's reward to us for surviving the cold and starvation. This was her sweet water, which was given from her breast for our nourishment.

I awakened Wàgosh and together we went into the forest with our axes. I did the notching and Wàgosh inserted the reeds into the openings and hung the birch pail underneath to catch the water. The birch vessels would stay on the trees and be dumped into clay pots to be taken back to the village. Hopefully we would get ten or more days of the sap running from the trees. When the women boiled the sweet water past the thick syrup, they then got the sweet brown granules that were added to our food over the summer.

Nokomis was also busy telling all the animals to bear their young in the spring. She then asked the earth to grow flowers to announce to all that the young animals would be coming.

As we were working on the trees and leaving the vessels to catch the water, Wàgosh wondered aloud if the Haudenosaunee would raid us this summer.

"Wàgosh," I said, "they have been busy raiding the Nippissing the last little while and bypassing us on the great river Kitcisìpi. Ever since we defeated them two summers ago with our friends the Innu (Montagnais) they have given us a wide berth. The Nippissing though are strong and the Haudenosaunee have to travel across many miles to raid and to steal the furs and the brown metal that the Nippissing get in trade with the Ojibwa. When the Haudenosaunee tire of the Nippissing they may turn their attention to us. However, until then we'll have to come up with a plan to handle them and maybe strike first. When we have our next visit with our friends the Innu and the Maliseet (Malicite), we will then have to decide something."

During the next hour Wàgosh and I notched all the trees that we had vessels for. After that we decided to try and find some fresh wìyàs (meat) or kìgònz (fish) for our families. We continued along our way toward the river. If we followed the river far enough up we would come upon a small stream that ran into the Kitcisìpi. Because the sap was late in coming this spring, the namebin (suckers) might start to run about the same time as the sweet water was ending.

"Mahingan," my brother said, "I think it is time that I thought of nìbawiwin (marriage)."

"My brother, you have to have someone to marry before you can do this. You cannot marry yourself."

With that Wàgosh jumped on my back and dragged me to the ground. I was laughing too much to resist. Wàgosh was also laughing and trying to rub my face into the ground.

"Brother, you know that I am in love with Kwìngwìshì (Gray Jay). I think it is time to ask her and her family if I can marry her."

"Wàgosh, I am happy for you and sad for myself, as Kwìngwìshì is outside our family, and I will lose you to their matriarch group. I will wish you all the best though, brother."

As we walked on toward the smaller river the woods were thick and the sun shone through in ribbons trying to melt the remnants of the winter's snow. Every step we took, we could hear the crunching of the last bit of snow that was hanging on underneath our feet. That, along with the sound of the wind and the birds, was the only sound of the forest. We walked silently and vigilantly until we heard the screaming of the pikwàk-ogwewesì (blue jay). With his warning we knew there was danger ahead.

9

BATTLE OF THE WOODS

WE WALKED SLOWLY TOWARD the sound of the jay. The warmth of the noon sun and our nervousness about the unseen ahead contributed to us sweating uncontrollably. If the jay was disturbed by another person we could be walking headlong into an enemy war party.

We came upon the small river in a short while and still the jay was yelling his warning. At that moment Wàgosh said, "I hear sounds, brother. They are the sounds of animals fighting."

No sooner had Wàgosh uttered that statement, but an immense stench permeated our nostrils.

"Mahingan, something has a shigàg (skunk) cornered, and he is not happy. There are a lot of smells in the air!"

"Wàgosh, I am afraid it is not a shigàg that is causing this horrific odour. Come. We will discover what all the noise is about."

We walked around a small bend in the river and came upon a rocky outcropping that led to the small river. Here we found what was making all the screaming and growling. Four kwìngwayàge (wolverines) had cornered an old bull moose as he was coming out of the small river. There was a mated pair with their two young kits from the previous spring. The old bull looked gaunt from a long hard winter that had weakened him considerably. The wolverines were a formidable foe at any time and the moose in his youth would have put up a ferocious battle and chased off this vicious pack, but not this day. They had attacked him when he was climbing the smooth rock from the river and the two adults were on his head, one on the nostrils and the other on the throat. The yearling kits were ravaging the bull's hind legs and had succeeded in tearing his back tendons away from his legs. The moose was bellowing, bleeding, and gasping for air. I could see the fear in his eyes, knowing that death was coming, and it would be slow, because the wolverines had not yet pierced his jugular vein.

Wàgosh and I watched the death dance for ten or fifteen minutes until finally the old moose bled out and died. The wolverines then dragged the old bull up the rock ledge to the edge of the forest.

Wolverines feared neither man nor beast in this wilderness, and they were as strong as they were vicious. It was very rare that we were witnessing a battle like this. Our elders told stories of the wolverine and their bravery and tenacity. There were few predators that would go head to head with them. However, hunger would make animals take risks.

"Wàgosh," I said, "I think it is time to go."

"No, brother. There is moose meat there for our taking!"

"Wàgosh, I would rather take on ten Haudenosaunee than try to take this moose from those killers."

As we were about to leave our hiding place down-wind from the kill, more players entered this battle-ground. The smell and noise of the kill had brought out the wolverines' biggest competitors, two wolves. They were young, probably only three or four, and probably had just become sexually active. There were only two of them, and because they were so young, it indicated they were starting their own pack. In all likelihood they had a couple of pups somewhere close.

The wolves wasted no time. They were hungry and the female had probably whelped seven or eight weeks previously so she was eating for more than one. They charged down the small hill at the wolverines.

Two full-grown wolves against two adult and two yearling kit wolverines was not very good odds, but hunger ruled. The wolverines, although caught off-guard, met their adversaries head on. The female wolverine immediately went for the throat of the female wolf. The wolverine, being so low to the ground, hung onto the wolf, and they tumbled and rolled down the rock embankment into the water. The wolverine then made quick work of the larger beast by holding onto her throat, weighing her down and drowning her.

The male wolf was close to death also. The female's mate had him by the nose and the two smaller wolverines were on the wolf's hind legs as they had been with the old bull. They were tearing him to pieces from the hindquarters and their father was tearing the wolf's face to bits. Soon he was dead. The wolverines had killed these two intruders in a matter of minutes with ferocity unparalleled in the wilderness.

"Wàgosh, do you still want to try to take some moose meat from them?" I asked.

"No, brother. I'm convinced. We'll see if the suckers are running. Fish will be enough for me today. Moose, some other time."

"Wàgosh, follow me. There is something I want to check out. These wolves had to have pups, and I would like one to raise."

We then skirted around the wolverines and their kills.

"These four will come back here for days to eat the moose and the wolves that they killed here today. Woe to another animal that comes here to feed if the wolverines are in the vicinity."

Wàgosh and I followed the trail that the wolves had left through the sparse snow until we came to a small den. I made the sound of a wolf calling its young, and instantly I received a small yowl in return. I had some meat in my pouch, and I set it outside the den. No sooner had I done this than a round ball of fur waddled out and grabbed the meat. I then grabbed him by the scruff of the neck and pulled the pup up in the air. He fought and squirmed, trying to turn his head to bite me, but to no avail. I noticed the pup was a male and had lots of fight in him.

"Wàgosh, I have a fierce companion now."

I then noticed he had a small bit of white on his nose shaped like a blaze cut on a tree like when we cut the sweet water trees.

"Your name will be Ishkodewan (Blaze), and if you grow up to be as energetic and brave as you are now, we will have many good adventures together."

10

THE AMIK

"WÀGOSH, AS WE WALKED from the ininàtig nòpimìng (maple forest) I noticed a pìtòshkob (pond). Let's check to see if there is an amik-wìsh (beaver lodge) there. This is a good time of the year for amik pìwey (beaver fur)."

"Mahingan, I have rope for the arrows so that when we shoot them, they won't swim away. It will be a nice treat to have some amikwànò (beaver tail) and beaver meat."

We walked back along our trail beside a small river. The day was getting warmer, and I could feel the warmth of the sun on my face and also the heat radiating through my furs that I wore. Ishkodewan was doing a good job of keeping up with us. I had tied a rope around his neck to pull him along when necessary and then when he tired I would carry him for a distance. He still tried to nip at me, but whenever he did I gave him a slap on the nose. He soon got the meaning of this and quit.

After a short time we arrived at the pond. Our plan was to take no more than two beavers. That way we knew there would be more in the coming years. The Omàmiwinini never take more than is needed. That way we never incur the wrath of Kitchi Manitou.

We sat by the pond and ate some dry moose meat we had brought with us. We tied the rope to our arrows and to our waist. When a beaver is hit with an arrow it swims down into the water and heads for its watery home. With the rope tied around our waist, we stopped their progress and then pulled them to shore where we could finish them off with our clubs.

After sitting for a long time, two young beavers broke out of the water. We had made sure that we were downwind, and I had tied Ishkodewan in the forest. We let the beavers get close to our arrow range. Our bows twanged simultaneously. Wàgosh's arrow hit his beaver on the animal's side and mine was below the head. Our ropes tightened as the beavers dove back down into the water. It was then a race to see who pulled their kill to land first. The loser would have to carry the carcasses home. Wàgosh beat me handily. Mine was a fighter and when I got him to shore, he charged me. However, I was able to club him before he bit me.

Then, laying the beavers on their back on a large rock, we cut the legs off at the first joints and then slit the pelt starting at the lower lip. Inserting our knives into this slit we cut the pelt down the belly to the vent. Working from this centerline and cutting with short strokes, we separated the skin from the flesh. Carefully, we pulled the legs through the skin, leaving four round holes in the pelt. We then cut off the tail. With great care we cut around the eyes and the ears close to the skull. Then removing the pelt and being careful to take as little fat and flesh as possible we laid the pelt on the rock and wiped off the blood marks with water.

We then proceeded to take out the scent glands from near the tail and the insides of the legs, being careful not to rupture the sacs. We would use these scents to bait our snare traps for other beavers and for the odjìg (fisher), a predator of the beaver.

The beaver tails and meat would make a fine feast for us. Wàbananang would be able to stretch and clean the pelts and make a warm coat or hat.

After finishing with the beaver I wrapped the meat up into the skins and tied everything together and slung it over my shoulders to carry back. Wàgosh and I then went back and retrieved Ishkodewan from the woods and fed him a piece of the meat.

"Wàgosh, on the way back we'll check the sap containers and dump what we have into our clay pots. Hopefully, we'll have enough for the women to boil today."

Upon reaching the maple forest we started to collect the sweet water. Then I heard an arrow whistle by my head and thud into the tree beside me.

11

MITIGOMIJ

WÀGOSH SNAPPED HIS HEAD around and yelled, "Brother, stop that!"

With that, the two of us turned around and out of the forest came Mitigomij (Red Oak).

"Brothers, if I was a Haudenosaunee you both would be dead right now!"

"Mitigomij, with you around we have no fear of Haudenosaunee. We know that you would have already killed them," said Wàgosh.

"Is that mishi-pijiw you call Makadewà Wàban (Black Dawn) with you?" I asked.

"Brother, there is only one way to find out, and that is to pretend to attack me."

Wàgosh then said, "We are not that foolish, Mitigomij!"

Mitigomij was my third brother. He was the best archer in our tribe and his power with a wewebasinàbàn (slingshot) was second to none. Mitigomij was also accomplished with the anit (spear), mìgàdinàn pagamàgin (war club), and mòkomàn (knife). He is a great minisìnò (warrior) and kigàdjigwesì (hunter), but our brother had one major problem that kept him from going on the warpath and hunting trips with us. Mitigomij would slow the party down. Twenty-two winters ago he was born with a pagamàgin ozid (clubfoot). Our brother had trouble walking for any length of distance and could not run at all. Because of this, he honed his weaponry skills to be the finest of all the Omàmiwinini. Our family unit and Algonquins all in all treated him as a special gift and all the great warriors and hunters taught him their skills. With these teachings Mitigomij became the best of the best.

When he was young, if the other children picked on him or teased him, he was quick to settle it in a decisive way. He always stood up for anyone being bullied and gained the respect and fear of his peers.

Travel on land was Mitigomij's biggest hindrance, but when it came to canoeing or swimming, no one in our band was his equal. As long as I could remember no one had ever beaten him in swimming, archery, or a canoeing contest. Many had tried. When the Innu and Malecite came for gatherings, they always brought their top warriors to try and defeat him in these contests. They were never successful. His upper body was the envy of all the young men. His one good leg was strong and healthy, but the leg with the clubfoot was withered. Because Mitigomij was so well treated by the warriors when he was young, he had taken it upon himself to be the self appointed teacher of all the young children for their weaponry and hunting skills.

When Mitigomij was twelve winters he came upon a panther that had a young male cub. The cub was black. A black panther is a melanistic variant and very rare. As rare as a white panther. He watched the mother and cub from a distance and the female came to accept him. Mitigomij observed as the mother killed game and brought it back to the young one. When the cub got older the mishi-pijiw took the cub on hunting trips and let him watch as she made her kill.

One early morning the mother was hunting and brought down a deer. The young male was lying in the woods watching and Mitigomij was at a distance. As the mother started to drag the kill to her cub's hiding place, a pack of several wolves came upon the panther and attacked her for the fresh kill. She had no chance and died defending her prey and her cub's hiding place.

Mitigomij knew that the cub now was defenseless and needed his help to survive. He got to the cub while the wolves were preoccupied with his mother. Then he grabbed him and took him back to the den.

For the next six or eight months Mitigomij brought meat for the young male. He never once brought him to the village. His thinking was that this was one of Kitchi Manitou's special creatures, and that he must leave him wild. With the help of Mitigomij supplying him with game, the cat became big and strong and totally devoted to my brother.

The cat would never show itself unless Mitigomij called him out of hiding. Makadewà Wàban was never far from my brother, always lurking in the shadows.

Mitigomij gained his warriorhood long before he ever took the Wysoccan Journey.

He was now twenty-two winters old, but when he was sixteen he proved beyond a doubt that he and Makadewà Wàban were not ever to be underestimated.

It was during the spring running of the suckers. Mitigomij was about an hour from the village along a small stream spearing the fish to bring home. My brother never strayed too far from the confines of the band because of his struggle to walk, but this day he went beyond his own boundaries. Where it would take us an hour to get somewhere, it took him two or three times as long.

Mitigomij was spearing and bringing in the suckers and every once in a while would throw one to the edge of the forest for Makadewà Wàban. Mitigomij was so engrossed in his task that he never noticed the four Haudenosaunee on the opposite bank, until Makadewà Wàban screamed a warning. They were young and probably out on a trek to find village locations or to capture lone people off by themselves in the forest. They travelled lightly for speed and effectiveness, living off of the land.

The four warriors charged across the small stream. Mitigomij threw his fishing spear at the lead warrior, catching the young man by surprise at the speed and accuracy of the throw. The spear entered his throat and exited halfway out the other side. He died in the stream, reddening the waters where he fell. When the next warrior reached the bank he was met head on by Makadewà Wàban, who knocked him down and started tearing at his face. My brother grabbed his war club from his belt and with the third Haudenosaunee upon him, broke the man's kneecap with one mighty swing. He then hit him in the face as the man dropped to his hands and knees. The last foe had only gotten three-quarters of the way across the stream. He was younger than the others, and he was terrified. He had just watched his three brethren killed before his eyes in less time than it had taken him to traverse the small waterway. Before Mitigomij had a chance to call him off, the panther splashed into the stream and ran toward the young warrior to make the last kill. Then with a mighty swipe of his paw, he shredded the right side of the foe's face. With a command from my brother, Makadewà Wàban stood in the stream screaming and snarling at the last Haudenosaunee.

Mitigomij then said, "My cat and I will let you live on this day. You go back to your people and tell them what happened here. I will leave your friends for the animals to enjoy. If I ever see you again I will kill you on sight. I will know you by the scar the black one has given you. Go!"

With that, the young warrior ran off downstream, leaving a trail of blood following him in the swift flowing water.

In the coming years, the story of the Omàmiwinini warrior with only one good leg and his Panther of Death spread among the Haudenosaunee. The Iroquois, we were told, skirted these woods since then because they said it smelled of death.

They told the story that it was Michabo (the Great Hare Trickster God), inventor of fishing, who was disguised as an Algonquin warrior, but had one leg that wouldn't change to a human appendage.

The Algonquin believe that they were made by Michabo. He also made the earth, fishing nets, water, fish, and deer. He lives where the sun rises and the souls of good Algonquins go to live with Michabo.

The Haudenosaunee also said that at that same battle Michabo was aided by Gichi-Anam'e-bizhow (The Fabulous Night Panther).

Gichi-Anam'e-bizhow was an underwater creature. To the Algonquins the underwater panther was the most powerful of the underwater beings. They believed him to be helpful and protective, but many times he was viewed as malevolent and brought death and misfortune.

The Haudenosaunee also feared that their men may have been killed by shape changers. This was an enemy who was to be feared beyond all else. Their powers were immense.

Mitigomij then awakened me from my thoughts.

"Wàgosh and Mahingan, I have not come to sneak up on you or to play games. There is something on the sìbì (river) that you must see!"

12

DANGER
FROM THE RIVER

BECAUSE OF HIS PHYSICAL limitations, Mitigomij had been given complete control as the village protector. He was responsible for all guard duties and overseeing the warriors for their sentinel duties. Most of the time, he did all the guard duty and only relinquished it when he was eating or sleeping. Between him and Makadewà Wàban the encampment was always well looked after. Thus, when anything out of the ordinary occurred, Mitigomij was always first on the scene to identify the danger and to make the appropriate decisions.

Mitigomij led Wàgosh and I with Ishkodewan following on a rope to the river. We had to be careful in our haste, so Mitigomij could keep up.

As we neared the river, we could smell the water. Mitigomij took us to a well-concealed vantage point. Off on the far shore and toward the shàwanong (south) we could see five or six canoes making their way through the sparse ice. Immediately I could see the danger that was approaching our lodges.

"Wàgosh, hurry to the village and have the women smother the fires with cedar boughs to keep the smoke down. Then send Kàg and Wajashk back to us. Send two young warriors to the epangishimodj (west) of the village. Have Asinwàbidì (Stone Elk) and the other two young warriors go to the wàbanong (east). You and Mònz go to the shàwanong, that way all the directions will have lookouts in case they have set warriors on the shore. Nìjamik and the other two elders will guard the village with the young boys."

No sooner than I had finished telling him, Wàgosh was off like a wisp of smoke on a windy day.

"Mitigomij, what do you think is going on?"

"Brother, it is too early in the spring for the Haudenosaunee to be raiding. If it is them, they do not have enough warriors in those canoes to come this far to raid the Nippissing. Because of the distance, I can't make out any markings on the canoes or see the warriors clearly enough to identify them."

"Mitigomij, if they were our friends they would not be on the other side of the river. It must be raiders of some sort, and they are on that section of the river to spot smoke from campfires. There's no other explanation. I really don't think there are any on our bank, but if there are, the village is on alert and well defended with lookouts on all sides, protected the best we can with the resources we have."

Kàg and Wajashk arrived well armed and wondering what they should do.

"As of now, we do not know what the threat is, but we will soon know who the object of our concern is."

In a short while the canoes were even with our position, and then we were able to identify them in the distance. There were six boats with twenty or so warriors. No women or dogs. They were definitely a war party, but why so few and why so early in the spring? But the biggest surprise was who they were. Hochelagans! They were from the island near the rapids of the big river. Hochelagans never usually wandered far from their fortified village. Their numbers were around twelve hundred but not strong enough to invade Haudenosaunee lands and they were always in fear of them. They had an ally in the Stadacona who lived upriver from them, but together they were no match for the Omàmiwinini or the Haudenosaunee in an all-out war.

"Warriors, let's go. I know what they are up to. Asinwàbidì, you'll have to go back to the village and tell the young boys to call in the sentries. Kàg and I will walk back with Mitigomij. When we get back, I will be sending runners out. There is a battle coming, and we will need more warriors than we have in our family unit."

By the time we had reached the village, all the people were assembled. They all listened intently as I spoke. "We have seen twenty of our enemy, the Hochelagan, going upriver. There is only one thing they are doing; they are looking for smoke from our scattered family units. I do not think they are here to raid as there are so few of them. I think they have come upriver to gather information of where our villages are and then to report back. This means only one thing — the Hochelagans are planning a huge attack in the very near future, possibly before the next moon. What we have to do is call in as many family units as we can and kill these men before they get back to their main encampment.

"My thoughts are that we have at the most two suns to gather. I am sending three runners out. Miskoz-i Kekek (Red Hawk) you will go to the west to the Matàwackariniwak (People of the Bulrush shore along the Madawaski River). Kinòz-i Inìnì (Tall Man) go south to the Kinònjepìriniwak (People of the Pickerel Waters below Allumette Island). Makòns you go to the Nibachi (near Muskrat Lake).

"My three runners, you have to leave now and travel with what daylight you have. You must reach our family allies by the high sun tomorrow, and they must join us by late dawn on the day after.

"Mònz, take Miskwì and Asiniwàbidì to the north and climb the high bald rock. There you will be able to watch the river for a great distance. You'll also be able to see for a distance along the shore where the forest fire went through along the river years ago. It's a very good vantage point. If you see anything, send someone back with information and stay out of sight and observe as long as it is safe to do so.

"Nìjamik, I cannot spare any warriors to go with you. You and the other two elders, Pijakì (Buffalo) and Andeg (Crow), will have to take the women, children, and young boys inland to the small waterfall that we go to in times of peril. It is well hidden and easily defended. Stay there until we send for you."

"Yes, Mahingan, I will look after everyone until your return," said Nìjamik. "May Kitchi Manitou watch over you and your warriors."

"Esiban and Agwingos, you must take Ishkodewan and look after him for me. Make sure you feed him and start his training to be a good hunting and guard dog. I'm depending on the two of you to take on this great responsibility in my stead until I can take over."

Within the hour the village was packed and gone. We kept three dogs for sentries, and they took the rest to help carry all their belongings. It would take them a full day of travel, but they will be in a safe place there. Our people had used this place many times when we felt threatened. There were caves, fresh water, fish, and game nearby.

With only Mitigomij, Wàgosh, Wajashk, and me left in camp, we settled back and waited for our Omàmiwinini brethren to come. It was time to paint our faces and pray to Kitchi Manitou.

13

THE ISLAND PEOPLE

I WOKE THE NEXT morning to the sound of rain on our lodge roofs with the accompanying thunder and lightning. This weather would help us in many ways. It would bring the Hochelagan canoes to shore, and they would be so anxious to make shelter from the rain that they may let their guard down.

We were constantly struggling to have enough to eat and always battling the elements to stay warm or dry. Add the constant threat of our enemies and it was a life of never-ending vigilance. Our whole survival as a nation depended on the health of our women. They cooked, looked after the children, maintained our lodges, prepared skins for clothing, and foraged for berries, fruit, and other food. When we brought game home, they smoked and dried it. They gave birth to our children with sometimes deathly consequences. Our future existence depended on the survival of our children. Kitchi Manitou had given the men the power to hunt and fish and make war. Nations waged war for two main reasons: to weaken their enemies and to capture women and children. With the capture of the women and children, the tribe could remain strong. Children grew up to be warriors and wives. Without either, the tribe would wither up and die like a fall flower. A community of men would die out eventually, but a village of women and children would survive and prosper because the children could grow and reproduce. While Nokomis fed all of us, the women were made in her likeness to carry on her work. When a man married, he always went to the matriarchal home. This was another reason woman wielded so much power. They brought warriors to the family unit, strengthening the village. The wife's mother was treated with great reverence and was never talked to directly by her daughter's husband. He and the mother-in-law had to talk to each other through his wife or another family member, never person to person.

Until then, I had not lost any of my brothers to another family unit. Mitigomij and Wàgosh were unmarried. Kàg's wife was captured in a raid on a Haudenosaunee camp many years ago when she was young. My wife, Wàbananang, was the daughter of Nìjamik. Mònz, our brother-in-law, was the son of Pijakì and married to our sister Mànabìsì (Swan). Kàg's first wife was of the Nibachis. A year after they were married she and their newborn son both died at childbirth. Kàg left his wife's family unit and came home to us. A couple of summers later, on a raid against the Haudenosaunee, he captured a young woman and brought her back to be his wife. Her name was Kinebigokesì (Cricket), the mother of the twins.

While Kitchi Manitou only gave us this land to oversee, we had to defend our interests. If someone else tried to force us off or threaten our families, we had to stand and fight. If we didn't and were submissive, we would be under their mìgàdinàn wàgàkwad (war axe) and have to suffer the consequences of any decisions our enemies made for us. That usually meant death or a completely different way of life than we had been used to, being their slave.

My thoughts were now on what the next few days would hold for us. Would there be death? These battles were always brutal because of the weapons we used — arrows and lances that tore as they entered the body. Hand-to-hand combat with knives that ripped and cut. War axes that broke bones and caused tremendous head wounds. If you were wounded and managed to live through the battle, you could bleed to death or die from infection if the Shaman or your fellow warriors couldn't get to you to administer the healing plants. If you were wounded and your tribe had retreated, you could expect no quarter from the enemy. All warriors were considered a threat. If captured alive, you were usually tortured or forced to run the gauntlet. And if you survived the gauntlet, sometimes you were adopted into the tribe or suffered painful retribution from your enemy. Surrender was almost always worse than death. The only time a battle was usually one-sided was when one of the opponents had been able to lay a successful ambush or if the numbers of one of the opposing forces totally outnumbered the other.

The life of the Omàmiwinini was forever between life and death at any known time. Cluskap, the Creator Force, had fashioned this life for us, and we had to accept our fate.

With the rain having let up a bit, we left Mitigomij to watch over the campfires. Wàgosh, Wajashk, and I went into the forest with our birch pails and collected the tree sap. We would store it in the village and when all this danger had passed, the women would boil the water down to the sweet contents.

The forest was laden with the smells of spring and the life that the rain was giving it. For me this was the best part of the year. However, another month or so and the pikodjisi (blackfly) would hatch. After the blackfly come the sagime (mosquito). Both drove men and beast to distraction. The giant moose and wabidì (elk) would be driven out of the forest into the lakes and ponds to escape the menace. My people used the crushed root of the goldenseal plant mixed with bear fat to keep these insects away.

We spent most of the day gathering the sap and storing it. When we were finished, Mitigomij had a meal ready for us.

Just as dusk approached, the rain and wind picked up with increasing velocity. With the weather starting to worsen, we headed for one of our lodges. At that moment the dogs started to growl, putting us on alert. Grabbing our weapons, we headed toward where they were facing.

"Mahingan, it's me, Asinwàbidì."

"Enter, brother. We have food and a warm lodge."

"Mahingan, because of the storm the Hochelagans have landed in the clearing. But there is another problem!"

"Yes, Asiniwàbidì, what is it?"

"There is more of the enemy than first thought. They have fooled us. The warriors in the canoes were a diversion. There was another force that had travelled through the forest on the distant river bank, and they have raided the Otaguttaouernin and taken captives. Wàgosh, they have Kwìngwìshì!"

With that Wàgosh jumped to his feet and grabbed his weapons.

"No, Wàgosh! We must wait for our people to come back. We are not strong enough in numbers to take on the Hochelagans until they arrive! If you go now they will leave with her and kill you in the process."

"Mahingan, my brother, you are right. I'll wait."

"Asiniwàbidì, how many captives and warriors do they have?"

"Mahingan, it was hard to tell, but at least ten or twelve captives, all women and children. Warriors, they have twenty from the boats and another twenty-five or thirty from the woods."

I then realized what had happened. "They must have left the other canoes down river on the eastern bank, then had those warriors continue on foot into the forest. That way when they were spotted on the river, their numbers didn't cause any concern. When they were past all the village fires, they ferried the group travelling on foot to this side of the river and started their raid. Their plans must have been to raid all the way down the riverbank area until they reached their canoes.

"Warriors, our plans have changed. We will let them raid us, thinking they have caught us by surprise. When our allies reach us, we will lay the trap. Hopefully this rain stays at this intensity, keeping the Hochelagans pent up until our brothers arrive. We can't risk attacking them. They'll have guards out and be on edge because they are in a strange land. The captives will be well guarded. They will do nothing until they can get their canoes into calm water. Our force will have to be split to handle their two-sided attack — land and water. Hopefully enough Omàmiwinini answered our call to make this trap successful.

"This will be our plan. All the fires in the lodges will be kept ablaze to make it look like we are all here. They'll probably attack in the early morning while we should all still be asleep. Their forces will come from the river and the nòpimìng (forest).

"They'll only have three or four men watching the captives. Mitigomij and Wàgosh will free them.

"Asiniwàbidì, go back to Mònz and Miskwì and tell them of our plans. As soon as the Hochelagans break camp, come to us. With luck on our side, the storm will hold another day, and we'll have more men."

The next morning brought the same heavy winds and rain. For us this was a good omen. Soon after we awoke and started the morning cooking fire, our allies started to come in. There was Minowez-I (War Dance) from the Kinònjepìriniwak with eleven warriors behind him.

From the Matàwackariniwak came fourteen men led by Pangì Shìshìb (Little Duck) and also with them were the two famous women warriors, Agwanìwon Ikwe (Shawl Woman) and Kìnà Odenan (Sharp Tongue). These two women were as skilled as any men in a battle. They were childhood friends. Neither of their families had any sons who had lived to warriorhood. When they were young, they proved their bravery in a great battle with the Nippissing and since then they had been accorded every tribute that went with being a warrior. They were constant companions, having made their home together, and neither had ever married. They were accepted by all in the Algonquin Confederacy of tribes.

Lastly, the great warriors of the Nibachis came into camp following Ajowà Okiwan (Blunt Nose). They were nine strong.

This gave our force thirty-eight warriors, plus our ten. Forty-eight total, enough to defend and win if my plan fell into place. When the warriors sat down to eat, they renewed friendships and past glories. Extra rations were given to my three young runners who hadn't eaten anything except dried meat since they had left.

Upon sitting down with Minowez-I, Pangì Shìshìb, and Ajowà Okiwan, we decided on our plan of action.

Minowez-I and Ajowà Okiwan would go to the river to fend off that force. Pangì Shìshìb and I would lay the trap at the village. It was agreed that Mitigomij and Wàgosh would rescue the captives.

Everyone knew that if one of us failed, it would bring disaster down on the rest of us. Surprise was of the utmost importance. Ironically, surprise was of the essence for our enemy also.

For now we passed the time painting our faces and chests, talked of past battles, bravery, and family while beating on our drums to summon courage from Kitchi Manitou. There would be death in the near future, and we would have to be prepared to confront it with bravery. The wind at the present resembled a small child's breathing and the rain was now a mist. We set out guards and everyone rested for the night.

Just as the dawn of the day was starting, I could hear the guards shout a greeting. Mònz, Asiniwàbidì, and Miskwì rushed into camp.

"Mahingan," said Mònz, "they have started to break camp and will be here before the sun clears the treetops."

With the news of the impending attack, I gathered everyone and told them to go to their spots. My group would go south of the village clearing. The dogs would have to be tied to stakes, or else they would follow us. The village had to have a habitual look, because if the enemy noticed there weren't any dogs it would arouse suspicion. With the rain coming down in a mist, the Hochelagans wouldn't expect anyone to be out. We made sure all the lodge fires were burning.

Everyone went to their places. The group led by Minowez-I and Ajowà Okiwan would be the most crucial part of the attack. They had to hold the force at the river, because if that faction broke through, we would be caught between the two Hochelagan forces with disastrous consequences.

While waiting in the forest, our bodies became wet from the rainy mist and our nervous sweat, and even with all this dampness I still could not keep moisture on my lips and in my mouth. The thought of an impending battle always brought out the weakness in a warrior. Death was not something that was looked forward to in this life, but it is an inevitable conclusion to living. We had to always go into battle knowing that we were defending our way of life and our families. Anything less in our thoughts would always bring out self-doubt, and with that came weakness. We painted ourselves for courage and to scare the enemy. Yelling and screaming as we entered battle relieved the tension and brought our senses to a state of euphoric intensity. I double-checked my weapons. Bow and quiver with fourteen arrows, one knife in my belt, another strapped to my right leg. My war club was in my belt with the rawhide wrist strap on the handle. This strap was important, because it insured I would not drop my club if I was hit, or if it was hit with another club. If it flew out of my hand it would stay attached to my wrist.

It was not long before we saw the first of the advance scout of the Hochelagan. Their bodies glistened in the early morning mist. There were three of them, but we would leave them alone. We wanted the main attacking force. If we killed this group of advance scouts it would warn the others of the ambush. The scouts stayed inside the tree line, avoiding the dogs' sight line and staying downwind from the animals. They vanished as quickly as they had come. The attack would soon occur, now that they had seen that the village was unaware and supposedly sleeping.

With the disappearance of the scouts back to the main body of Hochelagans, I was now able to tell our warriors the plans in more detail. We would wait until all of our enemies were in the village. As soon as they checked a couple of our lodges and saw that there was no one in them, they would know that something was wrong. I told the warriors to pick a target and wait until my bow sent its arrow. Then they were all to strike. With Mònz on my left and Kàg on my right, I felt a sense of calm over my body and I knew I wouldn't be harmed.

Within a few minutes, the enemy floated out of the forest like ghosts. They made no noise and threw pieces of meat to the dogs to keep them quiet. There were over twenty of them, and they walked furtively to our lodges. As the first ones looked into our homes, they realized something was amiss. At that moment, I let loose with my arrow and saw it enter the back of a warrior's neck. Almost instantly, twenty-six projectiles hurtled through the air and the screams of the Hochelagans could be heard in unison.

Pangì Shìshìb and I led our men out of the woods, screaming at the top of our lungs. I looked to my right and saw Agwanìwon Ikwe and Kìnà Odenan hammering down a warrior with their war clubs and Kìnà Odenan scalping him with her knife. Kàg's spear had only impaled his target in the leg, and now he was finishing the man off with another spear.

I soon returned my focus to what was happening in front of me. A brave with an arrow in his arm rushed at me with a stone axe. I was able to sidestep him and hit him on his wounded arm with my club. The force of the blow broke the man's limb. I now found myself behind my enemy and grabbed his hair, pulling his head up baring his neck, and in one motion I grabbed my knife from my leg strap and slit the man's throat.

In the forest from where the Hochelagans had entered, Mitigomij and Wàgosh were waiting for the battle to start before they made their move. Makadewà Wàban was close by and ready to pounce.

In a small clearing, there were seven women and as many young children held captive plus three Otaguttaouernin warriors who had already suffered torture at the hands of their captors. All of them had their hands bound, nooses around their necks, and were attached to the person in front of them. There were four men guarding the group and their attention was diverted toward the village.

At the first sound of screams coming from the battle area the men flinched. Then they started to laugh. With that Mitigomij's slingshot snapped and one of the men dropped to his knees with a huge hole in the side of his head. Wàgosh let loose an arrow and another man dropped. Before the other two knew what had happened, they were struck with a fury. One warrior had his neck broken by Makadewà Wàban's leap from a tree. The last Hochelagan turned to see Wàgosh descend on him only to meet with a crushing blow to his head by Wàgosh's war club. In a matter of minutes, it was all over and the element of surprise had brought the quick death of the four captors.

Wàgosh ran straight for Kwìngwìshì and embraced her. Mitigomij cut the warriors loose first. Even though their hands were missing a few fingers and their bodies had been burnt with coals and burning sticks, they did not linger. The three of them collected the weapons of the dead men and started to scalp and mutilate them in retribution for what had been done to them. While this was going on the captives were crying in relief at being rescued.

Quickly, Wàgosh and Mitigomij gathered everyone and brought all of them further back into the woods. If any of the Hochelagans tried to escape in this direction they did not want to be caught in this small clearing with all these defenseless women, children, and three very battered warriors.

At the sìbì Minowez-I, Ajowà Okiwan, and their nineteen warriors were laying in wait. They had decided that they would commence their attack as soon as the Hochelagans started to pull their boats on shore. The river was ten minutes away and hopefully the sounds of their battle wouldn't reach the village before they were able to attack.

The enemy came down the river in six canoes with eighteen warriors. As they neared shore, one man from each boat jumped out to drag it to land. The moment the boat hit land and the warriors started to pull the vessels up, Minowez-I and Ajowà Okiwan's men let loose a volley of arrows. Twelve of the Hochelagans were fatally struck, the other six in a matter of moments were overwhelmed and struck down. The battle was over in mere minutes.

All components of the Algonquin force came together after the battle. In total six canoes were captured, along with seven of the enemy and all their weapons. Many scalps had been taken. This was one of the most lop-sided battles the Omàmiwinini had ever participated in. The enemy had been totally destroyed, and we had only suffered a few minor scrapes and scratches. Our akandò (ambush) had worked to perfection.

It was decided that Minowez-I, Pangì Shìshìb, and Ajowà Okiwan could each take two prisoners of the seven that were captured, to do with what they wanted.

The captured women, children, and three warriors were all that was left of their village. They were given one of the captured men who had been the enemy chief. He would die a painful death of fire after running the gauntlet for what his warriors had done.

Myself, I was content to just take the canoes for our village.

Calling all the warriors together I spoke to them. "My fellow Chiefs and Warriors, we have won a great battle here today, one that will not be forgotten in years to come. Never before has a battle been so decisive and one-sided by an Algonquin force. It will be sung and talked about in our lodges for years. Now we will take all of the dead enemy warriors and pile them down by the river on a stack of wood and burn them. The stench of their bodies will travel in the wind to all our enemies, and they will know that the Omàmiwinini people are a strong and powerful nation. We will then throw their ashes into the river. Let it take them back where they came from."

With that, all our people let out a song for the dead of the Otaguttaouernin people who had lost their lives at the hands of the Hochelagans. That night we would dance and sing and torment our captives. In a few days our allies would leave to go back to their family units and I would send out runners to bring our people back. The existing members of the raided village would stay with us until the summer when all the tribes met to trade and talk in council. Then they would go back with another family of the Otaguttaouernin if they so desired. The surviving captives would pay for what they had participated in.

14

THE AFTERMATH

AFTER THE BATTLE WITH the Hochelagans, we sent hunters out to find game. They did not disappoint us, and came back with a moose and a deer.

We feasted, drummed, and danced for many days with our allies from the battle that had stayed to share in the celebrations.

The survivors of the Ottaguttaouernin village told us what they had suffered at the hands of their attackers. All their men had been killed, except for the three who had been rescued with the women and children. The Hochelagan captives were subjected to burning sticks and hot embers upon their bodies. Using clamshells we cut off their fingers to prolong their agony. If a warrior lost his fingers he couldn't draw a bow, hold a knife, or paddle a canoe.

The chief who had led the war party here was made to run the gauntlet. All the women and children of the raided village, our allies, and my family group lined up on two sides. We spread burning coals on the ground and stripped the chief naked. As he stood at the entrance to the gauntlet he sang his death song. When he was done singing, he started his run. Everyone in the line had sticks and clubs. As the man ran on the coals he was struck repeatedly by all the tribal members in line. The Hochelagan was a brave man. Not once did he cry out in pain. When he reached the end of the line he was bloodied from cuts and his feet were seared from the coals. We then gave him to the women, who took him and finished the job of torturing him until he died.

The women cut out his heart at the end, and it was given to the man who had captured him. The people then decided that the other six captives would also run the gauntlet. If they survived, we would then give them one canoe with two paddles and let them leave. Five of the Hochelagans survived. Very few of them had any fingers left and they all had been beaten and burned. The women cauterized their wounds, and then they took them down to the river, put them in a canoe, and shoved off. With few fingers on their hands to paddle, they would probably die on the river. If they didn't die and they did make it back to their village in Hochelagan they would likely starve to death, unless their relatives took pity on them and fed them. With few or no fingers they wouldn't be able to hunt or defend the village. They would become a burden to their people. It doesn't matter how good a warrior or hunter you were, if you ceased to be a person who could contribute to the well being of the village anymore, you were shunned. Everyone had to participate in the survival of the tribe. There are no idlers allowed. If somehow these men could make it back to where they were from and could help with the general welfare of the camp, they would survive. However, these men would still be considered outcasts. They came back as failed warriors. No fingers, no captives, no spoils of war and the loss of over thirty warriors in the land of the Omàmiwinini, branded as pariahs forever.

Failures like that would bring death and destruction on their village. No village could survive for long if it lost that many hunters and warriors. For a camp to survive the men had to be able to hunt. This was a bad omen to the conquered. It would be a long time before the Hochelagans would try to come to our lands again to make war.

In the course of the next few days Minowez-I, Pangì Shìshìb, and Ajowà Okiwan left with their warriors. Before they left, I told them there would be news about one of my family members in the next moon, when all the Algonquin tribes gathered for the summer meetings. With that I sent Makòns and Miskwì to bring back our women, children, and elders. Hopefully we would have peace for the summer and all would be safe.

15

THE WEDDING

THE BATTLE FOR THE captives and to save our village had been one full moon ago. Since that time all the
people had come back to the village and continued on
with their everyday lives. The men and boys were busy
hunting and fishing. The ogà (pickerel) were now running down the smaller rivers to the big river that we call
the Kitchi-Sìbì. The men would spear the fish from their
canoes or use weirs and nets. Women then made wooden
racks and smoked the fish over a fire. After this was done,
they dug a deep pit and covered the bottom with grass.
Then they put bark over the fish and filled in the pit. We
then had fish when we needed it. It didn't keep for a long
time in this pit, but long enough for our people to enjoy
the food for a month or so until we caught more.

When the Hochelagans had raided Kwìngwìshì's
village, they had killed her father and brother. Now all

that remained of her family was her mother. Wàgosh very much wanted to marry Kwìngwìshì. With the death of her father and brother, he really had no male to approach to ask permission. The three surviving warriors were not direct uncles but men who had married into her band.

Wàgosh approached Pijakì who was the village Shaman. He asked Pijakì how he should go about getting permission for his marriage to Kwìngwìshì.

Pijakì said, "Wàgosh, since Kwìngwìshì's mother Kàkàskanedjìsì (Nightingale) is not your zigosis (mother-in-law) yet, you can still talk to her directly. With no male relatives, I say that you can ask the mother, but if you do get married you will not be able to talk directly again to your mother-in-law."

"Thank you, Pijakì. I will ask her mother and hope for the best."

When Wàgosh approached Kàkàskanedjìsì to marry her daughter she did answer him — by saying yes.

When I found out that there would be a wedding I said to Wàgosh, "Brother, you have gained two women to do work in your lodge and the good part is you only will have to talk to one of them. How good is that?

"Wàgosh, because they have no close relatives or village family unit left, you will be able to stay with us once you are married. All my brothers will be close at hand. That makes our band much more powerful. Our band still has other women who will be getting married, and they will bring in more warriors who will strengthen our family division.

"Now, brother, I will send runners to the other villages to tell them that when we gather in another ten suns we will be having a marriage to celebrate along with the Minòkami Màwndwewehinge (late spring call together).

"I will also arrange for the hunters to go out and provide for this great feast! We will have to make some more fish weirs and nets. There will be many mouths to feed. You make me very happy, brother. I will announce to the village that my brother Wàgosh will take a wife."

Now that the wedding had been announced, the couple had to choose four sponsors who were older, well-respected people. The sponsors gave the couple spiritual and marital guidance throughout their lifetime. During the ceremony the sponsors pledged to help the couple.

Myself, I had taken on the responsibility of organizing the collection of food. I would have to send hunters out for wìyàs and kìgònz.

The first thing that I built was another fish weir. I built it at the mouth of the small river that emptied into the Kitchi-Sìbì. I placed a row of stakes in the riverbed, and then cut new growth reeds and weaved them together, leaving enough space between the weaves for the small fish to escape. We always made sure that we took only the mature, larger fish and left the young to grow and restock. This weir would catch enough fish in two or three days of the pickerel run to feed all the guests. Our women would be kept busy cleaning and smoking the catch.

The hunters would need to bring back at least twenty deer and lots of nika (geese) and shìshìb (duck) for the feast. For this job I asked Kàg and Mònz to look after obtaining the game. Since they would have to go far afield for the deer, Mitigomij would not be able to go with them. Instead he watched over the well-being of the village and took Esiban and Agwingos to the Kitchi-Sìbì to hunt geese and ducks.

Young men usually looked to their uncles for direction on how to be trained on the art of hunting and warriorhood. Fathers also led their sons toward what they had to become skilled at, but with an uncle there was more of an understanding and urgency about the skills that had to be acquired. Algonquin children were very rarely disciplined; it would have had to be a serious offense for them to be punished. The environment that they were raised in was harsh enough without their parents handing out punishment. From the time that they began to walk, males were versed in the art of hunting and girls in the chores of a woman. Young males were always playing games that tested their endurance. Boys were given a bow and arrow at a very young age. They used these weapons to play games of accuracy and to hunt small game. Young girls were given tasks in the village such as getting water, gathering wood, and picking berries. When there were skins to be made into clothes, they helped with that task also. They were taught to clean game and smoke the meat. Men were responsible for supplying meat and defending the village. Women fed the family, raised the children, made clothing, and packed up the camp when it had to be moved. Therefore it was very important that the children learned their jobs at a very young age. They were also taught to share their food, clothing, and spoils of the hunt.

From the time they were born, every day was a learning experience for all Algonquin children.

Weddings were always a time of feasting, dancing, and renewing acquaintances with other family units. It was also a joyous occasion for the village because they would be acquiring another warrior and hunter. The wedding took place under an arbour or in a ceremonial lodge. The couple committed themselves to the Creator, Kitchi Manitou. There was no breaking the commitment. The person who married them was known as the pipe carrier. They had to show total commitment before he would perform the ceremony.

Then the couple made a declaration that they wanted to be known as husband and wife. The pipe was lit and they smoked from it. Nasemà (tobacco) was then offered to and accepted by the pipe carrier.

With the day of the wedding only a couple of suns away, the Algonquin family units of the Kitcisìpiriniwak were starting to come to our village to erect their lodges. Wàgosh and Kwìngwìshì were busy making their clothing for the ceremony. With the help of friends and family, they were also engrossed in making gifts for the giveaway.

Once the ceremony was completed, the guests would all be invited to eat. First to eat would be the elders, then the pipe carrier, then the bride, groom, sponsors, and other guests. Any food that was not eaten would be given to the elders.

All the guests that came would be given a gift. The gifts were laid out on hides and the people starting with the elders down to the children would come forward to receive a gift of their choosing.

The joyful day commenced with the rising of the sun. Kwìngwìshì went down to the river to wash herself in order to be blessed by the spirit of the Earth. As the sun arrived at the top of the sky, the pipe carrier started the ceremony. Within minutes it was over and the drummers started. The guests started singing and dancing in honour of the married couple. The food was brought out and the festivities carried on. That night Wàgosh and Kwìngwìshì slept in a specially prepared lodge.

With my wife Wàbananang at my side, we feasted and danced throughout the night. The fires were kept burning brightly and the guests told stories of past heroic deeds and ancestors forever gone. The weshki-nibawidjig (newlyweds) had long since retired to their wedding lodge.

I was overcome with happiness that my brother had married and was lost in my thoughts as I watched the children play by the fires and the people drum and sing.

Wàbananang then held me close and whispered in my ear, "I am àndjig-o (pregnant)."

I turned and looked at her in the glow of the fire and kissed her on the forehead. "My wife, I am very happy. Life is very good!" I then started to feel the warmth of the fire and fell asleep in my wife's arms.

I awoke in the morning under the sky with a fur robe over me and my wife beside me. Standing over me was my brother Mitigomij with my wolf pup Ishkodewan licking my face.

Mitigomij said, "Mahingan, we have company coming down the river. They are not Omàmiwinini, but they have shown no aggressive tactics. They camped on the small island across from our village last night. I observed at least fifty chìmàn (canoes) and of what I could see in the diminishing light of the evening they were mostly warriors. I think they are Nippissing!"

16

THE CHALLENGE

"I DID NOT WAKE you Mahingan because they went right to the island and camped. I put all the other sentries on alert and told them to sound the alarm if they saw any movement from the island during the night. Because of the wàwìyeyano (full moon) and the cloudless sky, the island and waters in-between were well lit. If they had made any move during the night, the village would've been warned in ample time."

After Mitigomij's warning, I proceeded to wake the camp. The wedding had drawn eleven family units to our village, totalling about four hundred and fifty men, women, and children, of which there were probably about one hundred and sixty warriors. The families were staying together all summer for protection and to hunt and fish. Since we had wintered here, we would not stay another winter because the fish and game would be stressed by this many people hunting here. My group would transfer to another spot during the winter. The next spring we would travel to a site that another family unit had wintered.

Calling all the other family heads together, I told them that Mitigomij had observed a large party of Nippissing that had camped on the small island. I also told them about the small encounter that we had in the winter with the Nippissing warriors over the killing of the moose in their territory.

"Fellow family heads and chiefs, I do not think that our enemies from the north have come to wage war on us, because if that was their plan, they wouldn't be so obvious about their presence. I would imagine that they would send someone to talk to us soon. We will have to wait."

The other family units agreed with me that we should wait. The women brought us food. They had boiled us a meal of roots, kìgònz, and deer.

Soon after we had eaten, one of the sentries came to the village and approached where we were eating.

"Mahingan, Mitigomij says to come to the shore. Three chìmàn (canoes) have left the island and are approaching the shore."

With that, the group of leaders and I rose, grabbed our weapons, and left for the river.

I told the sentry to alert the warriors, but they were not to make any approach to the river unless we sent for them.

When we reached the river, the canoes were almost to the shore. Only one canoe approached and landed on the rocky shoreline. Three warriors were in the canoe, and they stepped onshore and approached. All were leaders and walked with no fear of us. One man was taller and more muscled than the others.

In a deep voice he said, "I want to talk with the Omàmiwinini warrior who has lost part of his ear."

Stepping forward, I said, "I am that person. Who are you?"

"They call me Mìgàdinàn-àndeg (War Crow). I am the chief of the South Nippissing Band. You and your hunting party killed two of my young men and severely wounded my nephew and another warrior."

"None of that would've happened if your young men hadn't attacked us. We would have taken our kill and left."

"He said your name."

"I am Mahingan of the Kitcisìpiriniwak. I lead many warriors!"

"Mahingan, I do not come to make war. Our tribes have always had small battles, and we remain enemies. We have never raided another's village in our history. I do not want an all-out war, but I want to test my warrior's skills against yours on the field!"

"Mìgàdinàn-àndeg, what do you mean by the field?"

"Pàgàdowewin (lacrosse)! We decide it on the field of pàgàdowewin!"

"Accepted. We will meet in two suns. There is a clearing a short distance from here where we can play. We will need that many days to find the mitigwàbàk (hickory) to make sticks for all our warriors. We have some, but I do not know if all are equipped. On the third day as the sun rises, we will meet you on the field. Send one of your warriors to us and we will show him where the field is. In the meantime, you will be allowed to send one hunting party of five men ashore to hunt game today. I am sure you have nets to fish, and you are welcome to that. We have nearly one hundred and sixty warriors to play. And you?"

"I have one hundred and fifty-four men with me. We are able." I then said, "What do we play for?"

"We play for hunting rights. If we win, you never come to our lands again. If you win, you are allowed to come only as far north from here where the battle of the moose took place. However, you will not win. We come prepared to teach you a lesson. Mahingan, you will feel the sting of the Nippissing skill on the field."

"We meet in three suns. We will play for two full days. The winner will be declared then. All injured players must leave the field. I will have the women build wàginogàns on the side of the field for the injured. During the two days before the competition, I will send out hunters also to bring in food for all competitors. We will play without break during daylight hours. If any warrior leaves the field during this time, they cannot return. We will each appoint one warrior to ensure this is adhered to. My brother Mitigomij will be our keeper."

"Mitigomij! A great warrior. Our people have heard of him. A good selection, he will be respected for his decisions. My choice will be my nephew who you almost killed. His name is Makadewà Kìkig (Black Sky). Until we meet in three suns, Mahingan, stay safe!"

When the Nippissing left, I turned to my fellow chiefs and said, "We will have to send hunters out to search for enough game to feed everyone the two days of the contest. In addition, we have to obtain enough hickory to make sticks for everyone. Our village has a few, but not enough. We will also need anìb (elm) bark and wìskwey (sinew) to make netting for the sticks. I will send the young boys out to find tree knots to use for the piwàkwad (ball). They may be able to find ten or fifteen, but even though they are the best pieces to use, they break easily. With this in mind, I will ask the women to sew some hide balls. These are a lot more resilient, but they do not fly as far when thrown from the sticks. Our young boys will also be in command of finding lost balls and bringing in new ones when the playing balls have been lost or broken."

When enemies had quarrels that they wanted to settle without bloodshed, or another tribe had a dispute that they wanted resolved, they could challenge their foes to pàgàdowewin. Our people consider pàgàdowewin to be a gift from the Creator Kitchi Manitou and a struggle between good and evil. Victory was always controlled by the Creator Force. This enabled both sides to settle the dispute without war. The game itself was a war, but without death. It tested all of a warrior's skills: running, agility, stamina, and bravery. When two foes played pàgàdowewin, they played for honour and to win at all costs. It was a battlefield with only sticks. No weapons were allowed. There were enough injuries as it was. An opponent was not allowed to hit another when he was down. A player could not hit the women or elders when they came out to take an injured player off the field, and they could not hit the young boys who looked after the balls.

At sunset, both teams retired to opposite sides of the field. There they would find food prepared by the women and firewood and shelter. The women and elders would take injured warriors to the side of the field that was designated for them. There their Shamans would look after them.

All our warriors looked forward to a game of pàgàdowewin. It is there and on a battlefield that they could prove their bravery and skill.

17

THE GAME

IT WAS THE NIGHT before the game and all the warriors gathered around a large fire to eat. I could feel the excitement among the men. The two warrior women, Agwanìwon Ikwe and Kìnà Odenan, insisted on playing also. They were among the fastest runners of all the warriors and were ruthless when it came to warfare or pàgàdowewin. All the other family heads and myself decided that we would start with the fastest warriors in the forefront. In the middle of the field, I would lead the young warriors. At the back, we would have the slower and stronger warriors.

During the day, Mìgàdinàn-àndeg and I had chosen two large boulders that took many men to move into position at both ends of the field. These rocks were to be the scoring posts. At both ends, an elder from each tribe sat to make the decisions on whether anyone scored.

They then would be responsible to mark a blaze on a cut tree that the elders had positioned beside one of the rocks. There would be a specially marked tree for each team. When you stood at one end of the field you could barely see the other end, it was that far. The field was also as wide as it was long. There were trees, stumps, and bushes that the warriors would have to negotiate around during the game.

The next day the oldest woman in the village came out to the middle of the field with the ball and laid it on the ground between Mìgàdinàn-àndeg and me. She then raised her hand in the air, and as I stood there in the field, I could feel the nervous sweat on my forehead. It seemed like an eternity before she yelled "go" and dropped her hand. With the sound of her voice, I swung my stick as hard as I could at the arm of Mìgàdinàn-àndeg. He blocked the swing with his stick and kicked the ball toward one of his warriors. With that, the game was on.

I ran after the warrior who had scooped up the ball, and at full flight received a hip from another Nippissing that sent me flying. The fall had ended with me in a small bush, the air leaving my lungs with a whoosh. By the time I had risen to my feet the throng of warriors was running toward our rock.

I watched as Mònz swung with all his might and caught the warrior who was carrying the ball square in the chest with his stick. The man dropped the ball and now Mònz had it. He ran directly up the middle of the field, knocking warriors out of the way with his hips and shoulders. At midfield, he tossed the piwàkwad to Kìnà

Odenan. She snatched it out of the air with her stick and ran off. A Nippissing warrior charged her with his stick wavering over his head. Kìnà Odenan weaved by him. As she ran toward the rock, Agwanìwon Ikwe came to her side. Two Nippissing then tried to get her between them, but Agwanìwon Ikwe clubbed the first one across the forehead and the second one she kneecapped. This enabled her close friend to near the rock. With over thirty Nippissing warriors chasing her, she swung her stick with an overhead motion and the wooden piwàk-wad hit the rock, shattering with a resounding thud. We had drawn first blood in many ways; Agwanìwon Ikwe had injured two warriors on the run and had set the tone for the rest of the day.

The Nippissing warriors then received a new piwàk-wad and the game continued. The piwàkwad carrier ran toward the centre of the field with at least forty warriors in front of him and behind him. The only way that we could get at him was to charge toward the horde of men running up the field. I led a rush of fifty players directly at the main body of the human wave coming toward us.

We met them about midfield with a resounding crash of bodies, sticks, and blood-curdling yells. A huge warrior knocked me into the air and I hit the ground with such force, my back felt like it had been realigned. Lying on my flipside, I could see the blue sky and every-thing going in circles. I knew that if did not get up in an allotted time the gamekeepers would force me to leave the field. I staggered to my feet and took a deep breath. Nothing was hurt but my pride. I looked around and at least fourteen or fifteen of our warriors and almost as many of the Nippissing were lying bleeding from head wounds or were disabled enough from other injuries that most of them had to leave the field.

I could see the Nippissing in the distance, and they still had the piwàkwad. With our people scattered over the field this turned out to be an easy score for the opposition.

I ran back to our end and told our warriors that we needed to run in a staggered formation up the field. The older warriors would lead on the offence and supply interference with the younger men and the two women being the ball carriers. When a Nippissing approached them, they were to hold on to the ball until the last moment and then pass it to the nearest open carrier. We needed to use our speed and cunning to combat the brute force of the Nippissing. If the Nippissing took the piwàkwad away from us, it was critical we attack them immediately so they could not form and charge as they did the last time.

With this plan, we advanced the ball up the field for most of the day, but were never able to get close enough to hit the rock. The enemy was always able to knock our ball carriers over and obtain the piwàkwad. We did score once and the Nippissing tried to run with all their warriors down the field as they had previously. However, we changed our tactics and instead of meeting them head on, we let the main body of players rush by us and then attacked the ball carrier from both sides. This worked extremely well, helping us to recover the piwàkwad and start our own rush.

The day advanced with both teams sustaining injuries. With darkness setting in, each side was probably down to about one hundred and twenty warriors and the Nippissing were leading us by two scores. With very little time left in the day, a group of Pangì Shìshìb's young warriors made a mad run down the field. With lightning speed and wild recklessness, they hit the scoring rock. With that final count, the keepers decided the first day was over.

I went to midfield and Mìgàdinàn-àndeg and I touched sticks to end the day. We retired to our respective sides of the fields to eat, sleep, and wait tomorrow's sunrise.

As I left the field, Wàbananang and my wolf pup, Ishkodewan, met me. My wife had a glow about her now that she was carrying our child. Kissing her on the cheek, she handed me a bowl of food and I sat on a robe she had put inside the lean-to that was set up near the field. She then left and went back to the village, leaving Ishkodewan and me. The wolf pup had grown a lot this summer and my two nephews, with my direction, had trained him well. Ishkodewan never left my side when I was around. Because the pup was too young to take on a hunt as of yet, I often left him with Esiban and Agwingos. The small dog, which had taken a liking to Ishkodewan, protected him from the other dogs.

With the wolf pup at my side, I was soon asleep.

I awoke in the morning to the sound of heavy rain. This would make the pàgàdowewin game more of a trial now. The field would be muddy and warriors would not have the footing they needed. I looked out into the field and observed large puddles of water. This made me smile. Today would be very interesting.

Our women had come back in the morning to prepare us food. My wife entered the lean to and handed me a bowl. The food was hot and I hoped that it would sustain me through the day. Once we were on the field, we could not leave for food or drink until the day was over.

Mìgàdinàn-àndeg and I met again at midfield to start the day. This time I won the piwàkwad and rushed down the field. With ten of our warriors leading me, I looked for one of the young warriors to pass off to. However, they were busy trying to knock down Nippissing warriors. I neared the rock and at least seven of the enemy were running toward me with one intention: to get the piwàkwad. Looking to my left, I saw a young warrior in the open. I hurled the piwàkwad to him and as soon as he received it, he sent it hurtling to the scoring rock. I was so intent on watching the pass and shot, I did not notice a huge water hole. I stepped into it, slipped, and then slid the length of it on my face. The water hole was not deep, but it was quite long and I skidded for an extended distance. This brought howls of laughter from both sides and all who were watching off the field. This embarrassing moment led to a change of play now for both sides. Whenever anyone was near water, players were trying to hit, shove, or trip the opposition into the muddy mess.

Halfway through the day, the field was a quagmire, with warriors from both sides either covered in mud or drenched from the rain. The teams were scoring at will now, because all the warriors were concerned about was whether they could dump someone into a puddle of water. It did not matter if they had the piwàkwad or not.

Luckily, no one had drowned yet. There seemed to be fewer injuries now because instead of each of the teams trying to whack each other with their sticks they were trying to push one another into mud or water.

This carried on for the rest of the day, and when Mìgàdinàn-àndeg and I met at midfield with the other chiefs, the elders told us the game had ended tied.

Mìgàdinàn-àndeg then looked at me and said, "Mahingan even though nothing has been decided, your warriors have proven themselves worthy opponents on the field of pàgàdowewin."

"So have yours, Mìgàdinàn-àndeg, I agree nothing has been decided. Kitchi Manitou has spoken and led us on another path. I put this to you before you leave; I will give you a mìkisesimik (wampum belt) to take to your people. This belt will tell what happened in the past few days and will signify a peace between our Nations. As you said when you appeared on our shore, we have been enemies and fought but only small battles. Never have we ever raided each other's villages. We have a common enemy in the Haudenosaunee. It is time to bury our differences and become allies. No more will we kill each other. We will respect your hunting grounds as you ours. If because of need one of us has to hunt in the other's homeland, we will leave an offering and only take enough to survive. If there is a common enemy, we will come to each other's aid. Tomorrow I will have a wampum belt for you to take back. If your people agree, send us a belt in return to seal the pact. When your answer comes back, we will smoke the sacred pipes."

"So be it, Mahingan. I will take this wampum belt back to my people, and we will send you an answer before the snows."

With that, the two Nations left the field and retired to their lean-tos to tell stories of the last two days. Our drummers and singers performed and our women made a great feast. Even though there had been no winner from the past two days, there had been an understanding that would help to ensure the future survival of the Omàmiwinini People.

As I sat down to eat, Esiban and Agwingos came running up to me. "Uncle, we have news of many pijakì!"

18

THE PIJAKÌ JOURNEY

THE PIJAKÌ ARE ANIMALS that the Omàmiwinini rarely get a chance to hunt. Only once did my father ever say that his people hunted this great beast, and he was a very young boy at the time it happened. These beasts were only able to come near our hunting grounds when the big lake completely froze over during the winter. This enabled the animals to walk across the ice from the south, looking for grass and salt licks. They then would be here until the next winter, disappearing from our hunting grounds when the lake froze over again. When the big animals appeared, it was a time of great happiness. Slaying these huge beasts would keep many stomachs full over the winter.

The women dried the meat over fires and then mixed it with berries. We then stored the food in baskets for later use. The Omàmiwinini always considered the coming of the buffalo a reward from Kitchi Manitou.

Esiban and Agwingos said that they had talked to a Wàbanaki (Abenaki) warrior who had come to tell us of a great herd that was near the big lake. He was now eating in our village and the man said that he would lead us to where the herd was. His people had sent him to ask for help in herding the great beasts into a wìbwàte (corridor) and then into an enclosure where they could be killed by the warriors. The corridor would be made of fallen trees and rocks built along two sides tapering into the enclosure, backing onto a large hill with stone on all sides. Once the animals were in the penned area, we would shut the entrance.

Buffalo supplied many things for our people. The animal was bigger than a moose or a wabidì.

Besides the meat and the hides, we used the sinew for thread, bowstrings, and sewing. The people used the bones for tools, knives, arrowheads, and pipes. Horns were used for eating utensils, the hair for rope, the brain for tanning hides, fat for hair grease, and the stomach and bladder for water containers and cooking. Nothing went to waste.

With so many families encamped for the summer, there would be many hands to help in this hunt. Upon talking with our visitor, we decided that the main body of the village would leave in a week. It would take us that long to make the wìgwàs-chimàn (birch bark canoes) that we would need to transport the people there. Then after the hunt, we had to bring the meat back. It will take only four or five suns to reach where we had to go. As many warriors as possible would leave the next day. Then, once they arrived, they could help in the making of the corridor with our Wàbanaki allies. When the women and the rest of the men arrived, the hunt would be ready to commence. We would need the skills of the women to cut up the animals and prepare the meat and hides for the journey home.

First we had to make the birch bark canoes that we needed to transport us. After the two-day game with the Nippissing, about thirty of our warriors had suffered enough injury to prevent them from taking the journey. They would stay with the elderly and the young in our summer encampment, while the rest of the village participated in the hunt. Among all the family units we had fifty-four canoes that were available to leave immediately. With a hundred and thirty warriors and another two hundred and twenty women and children to help with the slaughtering of the animals, we would need a hundred-and-twenty-five canoes. With what we had already, we still needed another seventy vessels.

The next morning a hundred and sixty warriors, women and children left on the journey accompanied by the Wàbanaki warrior. The rest of us would follow as soon as we made the remainder of the boats.

We started immediately to build them. All the other family heads except for Minowez-I and me had left with the first group. Wàgosh, Kàg, Mònz, and their families had also gone with them.

Mitigomij had stayed with me and we would travel in the second group.

The remaining men were gave the task of cutting cedar for the framing of the boats and large birches from which we would peel enough bark to cover each canoe.

They would then build the vessels on a sand beach near the village. The women and children had the assigned job of digging up the spruce roots that we needed to bind the wooden parts of the canoes and the sewing of the bark skin.

Once all the materials were collected over the course of a couple of days, the men started to make the gunnels, ribs, and plankings from the cedar using an axe and a crooked knife to shape the curves in the ribs. The bark and the spruce roots were then placed in the river to keep them fresh.

The ribs that we had cut from cedar also had to be soaked for a couple of days and then boiling water poured over them to help with the bending. The people next rolled the bark out on the level beach, the frame weighted down with heavy rocks, and then the bark sides turned up. Afterward we set the assembly to the proper height and had everything lashed together with the spruce roots. To seal the canoes, we used spruce gum and animal fat.

While the canoe building was going on, the young boys, under the direction of Mitigomij, cut trees down and took them to the elders and the injured warriors who then made paddles. Everyone worked from sunrise to sunset to get as much done as possible. On the days that it rained, we still worked on the boats.

After nine days, we had sixty-eight boats finished and ready to float. We were ready to leave. Two-hundred-and-eight of us prepared for the journey.

Because Wàbananang was with child, I decided that she should stay behind. Thirty-one warriors who had varying amounts of injuries but nothing life-threatening, forty-two elders, twenty-five pregnant women, and the young children would be staying behind. We would be gone for at least a moon on this trip. I hoped that all would be well with the people that we had left behind.

I turned to Mitigomij and Minowez-I. "The time has come to leave. We must get everyone organized and the canoes loaded. Mitigomij, will that wild cat of yours be able to keep up on the shore?"

"No problem brother. I hope that wolf cub of yours can swim if he has to!"

We decided that we would take the Wajashk Sàgahigan and Sìbì (Muskrat Lake and River) system down to the Kitchi-Sìbì and miss the biggest onigams (portages). We would come out to the Kitchi-Sìbì before the big bend and have to portage there. We would have seven sets of rapids to go around and one set that we could ride through. This would take us four to five days to reach our destination.

When we left, Mitigomij, Ishkodewan, Minowez-I, his son, and I were in the lead canoes. After we had been on the river for a while, I looked back at the boats; it was an amazing sight to see sixty-eight boats and all the people. If this hunt were successful, our winter would be one without hunger pangs and starvation for the old, the weak, and the young. The hunt would strengthen the Omàmiwinini for years to come.

Travelling with this many people, we had to be concerned with feeding everyone. A decision was made that when we did an onigam, the women would prepare food as the men portaged. After all the canoes had cleared the portage, we created a pagidjiwanàn (resting place on a portage) and ate.

Minowez-I and I had also decided that while we were travelling on the river, all of the women and children who were not paddling were to troll for fish. Anything that they caught would be filleted right in the boat. They then used the entrails for more bait. This gave us enough food to eat, along with any roots and berries they found when we stopped.

At the end of our first day, we had made two portages. On the first one the women quickly got cooking fires going and the children who we had brought with us foraged for berries and roots. By the time the men had finished the portage, we could eat and rest. The women also made everyone lots of hot kìjik anìbìsh (cedar tea). This drink kept everyone healthy and strong. The second portage was a longer one. Minowez-I and I had decided ahead of time we would camp here for the night. With that in mind, we sent a couple of hunting parties out and had warriors make lean-tos for shelters. The women gathered wood, made fires, and started meals. The rest of us made two or three trips each carrying canoes and other supplies.

The hunting parties that we had sent out came back with a couple of deer and a few rabbits. The women made a very good meal of all this. After all had eaten, I asked Mitigomij to meet with Minowez-I and me.

"Mitigomij, we would like you to oversee the security of the camp when we stop each night. We know you cannot help to carry the canoes when we portage, so we will leave it up to you and any of the young warriors of your choosing to be camp guardians while the canoes and supplies are being moved overland. We respect the vigilance that you and your panther friend Makadewà Wàban have shown toward our safety at all times. Even though you have limitations, we never doubt your courage and warrior skills."

"Minowez-I and Mahingan, I will defend our people to my death. I am proud that you think enough of me to take control over the camp security. Makadewà Wàban and I will not let you down."

We had also brought twenty-three of our dogs to help with the hunt. It was the job of the children to care and feed for them. Each child had one dog to care for. It was the young person's responsibility to ensure the dog stayed in the canoe with them on the trip.

After two days, we had made it to the Kitchi-Sìbì and past two more portages. As we were paddling, I mentioned to my brother what I had in mind for him.

"Mitigomij, you know that once we get to the hunt you will have to stay with the canoes and guard them. You wouldn't be able to keep up with us as we travel inland to where the buffalo are."

"Mahingan, I know this and I accept my way in life. My tasks are always important for the survival of our people, and I do not perceive my disability as a detriment, but only as a sign from Kitchi Manitou that I am destined for other paths in life."

"I will leave with you some of the younger boys who can help with the fire and keep watch. You have Makadewà Wàban who is equal to five warriors. I do not expect any trouble from the south, but we must be observant."

With the ending of the day, it was not long after everyone had eaten that all, except for the sentries, were asleep. Ishkodewan, who had grown a lot since I found him in the spring, always slept next to me. Still a young wolf, he was eager to learn when I took him on a hunt. Obedient at all times, the animal was developing superior hunting skills through the teachings of the small dog and me. The two of them were inseparable while hunting and or when in the camp.

When we awoke the next morning, there was a misty rain. Today would bring us to the end of our journey, but there still was one more set of rapids to take.

"Minowez-I, we will have to keep the canoes well spaced when we go through the last set of rapids. We do not want any of the boats bumping into each other causing them to capsize. Mitigomij and I will go first and you and your son can send the others at intervals. We will land on the west shore and when you send the next one they will land on the eastern shore. That way if anyone overturns, there will be someone on either shore to help them."

"Okay Mahingan. My son and I will control things from here. Don't worry about us."

Mitigomij, Ishkodewan, and I started on our descent through the rapids. The misty rain moistened our faces and the roar of the fast moving water made my heart race. As we looked toward the white water, the movement made it look like the river was waving us on to make the journey. Taking this as a good omen, we started our descent down river. We could feel the power of the river beneath our boat. The only sound besides the river was my wolf cub growling and snapping at the water as it washed over the canoe, soaking all in the boat. With the helpful skills of my brother, we rode the rapids and arrived safely but wet on the shore.

As the morning wore on, all the boats made it through the rapids. When we did have a couple of spills, no one suffered any injuries, as we pulled the overturned occupants to shore with the empty canoe. We had now split up on the two shores and both sides had fires going to dry our clothes and to make a meal.

The last chìmàn to come down the rapids were Minowez-I and his son Nigig (Otter). Since everyone was safe, this was the celebratory voyage of the rapids. They put on quite a show, shooting the river at the most turbulent spot and flying through the air. Father and son both had huge smiles on their faces. During the last stretch of rapids, Nigig stood up in the front of the chìmàn with his arms spread out and the spray drenching him as Minowez-I steered the canoe. Everyone was yelling on both shores and urging them on. When they reached the shore, they arrived to whoops and cheers. It was a fine ending to a safe trip through the rapids.

For the rest of the voyage the river was calm with a slight breeze and no incidents. Near the end of the day we came upon two canoes with young boys and elders in them. They led us to a sheltered bay where our people who had preceded us had come ashore. Several older Wàbanaki and Omàmiwinini children as well as some elders watched over the canoes. They were very excited to see us, and we soon renewed old acquaintances with the Wàbanaki elders.

They told us that most of their hunters were camped about a half-day's walk away. With darkness approaching we decided to spend the evening here and before long the women had the fires roaring and a meal prepared. That night we listened to stories from the Wàbanaki elders of long ago wars and successful hunts. The stories went on long through the night before everyone decided to make their beds and sleep.

The next morning I sought out Mitigomij. Embracing him, I said, "Brother, I know by the time this hunt is over and everyone comes back to the canoes, all these young boys who are staying here with you will be trained in all matters of hunting and warfare."

"Mahingan, you overestimate my skills."

"Never, my brother. There is no one who I would rather have beside me in battle than you and that panther. Good luck and I will see you in seven or eight suns. If there is trouble, send the twins to us. They are fast runners."

"Mahingan, there won't be any trouble that I can't handle!"

After everyone had eaten, one of the Wàbanaki elders said that he would lead us to the camp where the hunt would take place.

Minowez-I and I walked in the lead with the old man. During the trip he told us about the last time that our two peoples had hunted the buffalo.

"It was many years ago, I was a small boy and our two tribes had then also joined together for the hunt. The buffalo had come over the river in the land of the Attiwandaronk in the dead of winter. During that spring, the Ouendat (Huron) had hunted them, driving them to an area we were now travelling to reach. There were many animals in the herd. One of our elders said that he had a vision and in it, Nokomis came to him and told him that an animal that we had never hunted before would come to our lands. She told him that this great beast's meat would feed us for many months and supply our people with items that we could use in our everyday existence. There was only one thing we could not do; we must not kill the entire herd. If we took just what we needed, Nokomis would send them back when we needed them again to stave off hunger.

"She has kept her promise. They are back."

19

THE GREAT PIJAKÌ HUNT

AS WE WALKED, MINOWEZ-I and I talked about how impressive it was that we could organize everyone for this hunt in such a short amount of time.

"Our people are very resourceful when they have to be, and they have proven it by this journey here. Let's hope the hunt will be as successful as the trip here was," said Minowez-I.

We arrived at the campsite by noon and soon settled in. The people erected lean-tos for the men and some wàginogàns for the women. The temporary village was huge with over six hundred warriors, women, and young boys. After eating, we convened a council and our scouts pointed out the herd was about a day from here, and they had not been disturbed. They were roaming toward the river and grazing. The warriors who had preceded us had almost finished constructing the corridor where we would drive the animals down. There were close to a thousand buffalo. It would take about two more days to finish the trap, and then we could start driving them into it.

After the council, the family heads called our people together. We had decided we needed another twenty or more canoes for the trip home. The women and boys agreed to the assignment of making them, plus travois to carry the meat. Much work had to be finished before we could start the hunt.

After two days the trap and corridor was finished. The place where we were planning to drive the herd was a small valley with a large bluff that the animals would not be able to scale. Along the sides of the final enclosure the men had angled sharpened poles propped up on logs and weighted down with rocks. This would prevent the buffalo escaping by pushing against our barriers.

That night we danced, drummed, told stories of past hunts, and prayed to Kitchi Manitou to watch over us and to make our lances and arrows fly true to the mark.

From what the scouts had told us, these animals were huge. The warriors would have to take care and not fall under their hooves, because it would mean certain death. Leaving that next morning to start the hunt, we had to make sure that we stayed downwind as long as we could so that the animals would go in the direction we needed them to pass through. The warriors then lined up on both sides of the corridor to keep the animals on course, waving robes and yelling. The chiefs selected one of the warriors to be the caller, trying to lure the great beasts to the open end of the path we wanted them to travel. One of the Wàbanaki elders had an old buffalo robe for the caller to wear and, using this ruse, he imitated a calf in order to draw the herd toward the corridor.

After sunrise, the warriors ate and were keen to start the hunt. The women and young boys stayed on the top of the bluff until we had the herd in the corrals, and then they would come and help with the butchering. Including the Wàbanaki warriors, we had over two hundred men for the hunt.

Wàgosh, a few other warriors, and I had volunteered to bring the dogs and Ishkodewan. We would let them loose once the caller had the herd moving, and they would then chase the buffalo toward the corridor. With beasts as large as these, it would be a challenge to direct them to where we wanted them to go.

"Mahingan, do you think the buffalo are as big as the scouts say they are?"

"The scouts say they are bigger than the moose and elk that we have hunted since our fathers. I have only heard of one other time that Kitchi Manitou has sent these animals to our lands and when those stories are told it is said that they were huge."

We walked for most of the morning until one of the scouts met our small group and told us that the herd was ahead. We had to veer off to the north to stay downwind from them. By midday, we had found them. It was now time to organize all the warriors to where we wanted the herd to be driven. The buffalo were grazing in a meadow and had not caught wind of us. The chiefs directed the men to their spots. The hunt would commence at sunrise; we did not have enough time left in the day to start.

Wàgosh and I stood on the high escarpment that we had camped on and watched the herd.

"Wàgosh, fill your mind with this sight. We will never see anything like this again. The buffalo does not call the land of ours home. They are here by mistake, and we will never get the opportunity again in our lifetime to hunt them."

"Mahingan, they are huge!"

During the time we watched them we could see huge bulls fighting for the breeding rights of cows. Most of the time the fight ended after a few charges and head butts, but there were times when a bull gored another and drew blood. The bulls continually were bellowing and sending chills up my back. What a magnificent beast; they would certainly challenge all our people's skills tomorrow.

With the rising of the sun, we hurriedly ate and readied our weapons. The time had come. Even the dogs were restless; they knew something was about to happen that was to include them. I called my wolf over and stroked his head.

"Ishkodewan," I said, "Today you will hunt a giant. Good luck, my friend."

The herd started to move toward where we needed them to travel. The caller was doing his job. We then took the dogs to the rear of the herd and let them loose. There they started their frenzied barking, and with the warriors shouting and waving, the beasts broke into a run. They funnelled toward our corridor and all along both sides warriors yelled and waved. Once the animals passed them, the men joined in the chase. The cows were leading the panic, with the bulls running behind them and the younger buffalo bringing up the rear.

By mid morning we had them in the corridor where we had made our barriers. In a very short time they were in the corral and the killing began.

Just before reaching the bluff, one of the Wàbanaki warriors came too close to a bull. By the time anyone realized what had occurred, the bull had gored the man and the rest of the wildly running animals trampled him. After the herd had passed, his broken body laid on the trampled ground — a sacrifice to what was about to happen.

Now that we had the buffalo corralled, the slaughter began. The sounds and sights of the buffalo frothing and bellowing, the warriors yelling, and the dogs barking were deafening and terrifying all at the same time. There was so much dust and mayhem that you feared for your life at all times.

Wàgosh and I stayed together and fired our arrows into the lungs and hearts of the beasts. When an animal went down, they let out a huge gasp of air and blood flew out of their mouths and nostrils. Once I looked around and saw Mònz with his spear driving it into a cow. The animal dropped to its knees and Mònz drove another spear into its lungs. By this time he was covered with blood and yelling his lungs out.

Wàgosh turned to me and said, "Mahingan the stench of death is overpowering here today. I have never experienced anything like this in my life before. It is overwhelming!"

"Yes, Wàgosh, but it also is the sweet smell of life for our people this winter. Our women and children will have lots to eat and our elders will not suffer the pangs of hunger and die because of their weaknesses. This animal is giving us a chance to make our children stronger through his life-sustaining meat. Sometimes the stench of death means a new life for something else."

The killing took place for most of the afternoon. When the family heads had decided we had enough for all, the rest of the animals were set free. I called for Ishkodewan and he and the small dog came on the trot, both of them covered in blood. He had learned about the hunt today and the dogs would eat well for the next few days.

I looked up to the top of the bluff and saw all the women, young boys, and elders cheering and waving. Soon they were running down to the killing area.

We would all have to work hard now, butchering and getting all this meat back to our camp on the upper Kitcisìpi Sìbì. There would be travois to pull, and then there were the extra canoes that we would have to carry out to the river where Mitigomij waited for us.

It was several more days before we started for home, as we wanted to take as much meat as we could and not leave any behind if we could avoid it. It took a tremendous amount of planning and extra work to get everyone home. The journey here was easy; we did not have the extra weight of the meat.

There was also the worry of our most feared enemy, the Haudenosaunee. We were near their lands.

20

THE RIVER HOME

NOW THAT THE HUNT was over, our people gave thanks to the animal's spirit for its sacrifice, enabling us to survive.

After the ceremony, everyone started working at their tasks. The warriors had the responsibility of making the rest of the travois for all the men and women, plus smaller ones for the dogs. The canoes were finished and we sent a group of warriors to take them back to the river. They then had to return to help carry the meat out.

The women placed the buffalo on its side with the help of the warriors. They then tied rope to the animal's feet. This let them roll it into position to butcher the beast. The women then cut the buffalo down the belly and took off the top half of the hide, cutting away the meat from the bones. They then tied the rope to the feet and flipped the animal over to continue the other side.

The big bulls were hard to move so they placed them on their bellies, with the legs spread. They then cut across the brisket and neck, folding the hide back so they could cut the forequarters at the joints. The women next split the hide down the middle.

After cutting the meat off the bones, they put it on drying racks to preserve it. Our people put to use every part of the buffalo. We knew that this great beast might never come this way again and the people had to make the most of this stroke of luck.

After the hides were cut off, the brain of the animal was used to tan the skin by rubbing the under surface and then staking it out in the sun to dry.

After about four days the stench of the dead animals was stifling. This brought the crows, ravens, and turkey vultures who were trying to get their share, in company with the coyotes and wolves that were lurking around. Chasing all these scavengers away kept the camp dogs busy day and night.

While the women were doing the butchering, warriors were carrying what they could to the canoes. It was at this time that a meeting of the family heads convened.

"The warriors who have been carrying meat and robes to the canoes tell me that maybe they should start off for our summer home with what is already loaded. I agreed with them and came up with a plan to help us speed up the journey home for everyone. They say that in the next day they will have forty-five canoes loaded. My suggestion is to send ninety warriors home. There is still several days' work here to do. If we wait to finish, the trip home will be cumbersome with one hundred and fifty canoes and only one hundred and thirty warriors to help paddle. The warriors say that they can make the round trip in nine or ten days. When they return downriver, they will be able to meet our people as they are returning and help them from there."

"Mahingan," said Pangì Shìshìb, "if we send ninety warriors home, we will be left with only forty men. What happens if the Haudenosaunee arrive?"

"Our scouts tell us that they have not seen any activity from across the big lake, plus the Wàbanaki will be here until the end. It is an easier trip for them because they will be going with the current of the big river home. After the ninety warriors leave, we will be leaving in groups of sixty-five, including ten warriors, in twenty-five canoes over the next several days. As the ninety start to come back to us, they will be able to relieve our loads and give us extra manpower in the canoes.

"I see your plan now, and it is a good one," said Pangì Shìshìb.

"Do we all agree then on the final plan?"

"Yes, Mahingan," they all said in unison.

"Fine, let's get started. The ninety will leave now."

Over the course of the next several days, all the groups left. My group was the last one. I had nine warriors with me. There were my three brothers, the two warrior women Agwanìwon Ikwe and Kìnà Odenan, Minowez-I, his son Nigig, Makòns, and Miskwì. Furthermore, we had fifty-five women and young boys divided into twenty-five canoes.

"Mitigomij, we are finally heading home."

"Yes, brother, but I have a feeling that the Haudenosaunee will still make their presence felt. We have to be cautious and anticipate that a few of the ninety will reach us in good time."

Wàgosh and Nigig, who were standing near Mitigomij and me, also expressed their concerns of our enemy from the south.

"Don't worry. Kitchi Manitou has been with us up 'till now. He'll watch over us until we are safely home."

The first day of our trip home was uneventful. We divided the warriors among ten of the canoes. Each warrior's canoe had a young boy in it. The other fifteen canoes had three paddlers each, mostly women. Four of the warrior canoes took the lead, two in the middle and the final four safeguarding the rear boats of the small group. The warriors had been positioned so that if there were any trouble they would be near by to lend a hand. In my boat, I had a boy named Pashkwadjàsh (Coyote), the small white dog, and Ishkodewan. The boy was the same age as the twins and asked many questions about the sìbì. He was good company and a strong paddler. His father was one of the ninety warriors who had left nine days ago. The boy's mother did not make the trip because she had a very young daughter to care for that was born last fall. Each canoe was loaded with as much meat and robes as it could handle. Near dusk, we portaged at the big rapids and made camp. Sentries were posted, and for watchdogs they had my wolf and the small dog. All was well so far.

The party awoke the next morning to rain. We decided to continue, but if the winds came up we would head to shore. We travelled until our next portage and stopped for the day as the weather had worsened.

At this encampment, there were lean-tos from our previous trip downriver. There we waited out the weather and stayed dry. The next morning would hopefully bring a break in the conditions.

The following day the weather started to break. The plan was to eat and then with a bit of luck we would be able to leave before the noon sun. The ninety had been gone ten days now. In the next day or two, the first couple of groups would start reconnecting with the returning warriors. With the extra boats and labour, this would hasten their return trip. Our expectation was that we would see the warriors in a couple of days. The four groups that left after the warriors would not make very good time. With only ten men in each group, the portages would be time consuming. We would have to make many trips during the portages because of all the meat and robes that were in each canoe. The women were an immense help but could not carry as much as a man. We kept a few travois to help us with the transporting of the buffalo meat and the robes on the portages, but it was still a burdensome time.

We were able to get away before the noon sun and calm water ensured the easiest travel since we had started the trip home.

After we had been out on the river for quite awhile, Mitigomij doubled back with his canoe.

"Mahingan, Makadewà Wàban has appeared along the shore twice. When he shows himself like that, it only means one thing. He sees something he does not like. Someone must be following us!"

"Mitigomij, there is a big bend in the river up ahead. We can put ashore there, and then we will be able to look back onto the river for a great distance. If anyone is following us, they will come into our view at that spot."

As soon as we reached the bend, we told the rest of the people to continue. We did not have to wait long. Down the river, we could see boats appear.

"Haudenosaunee, my brother?"

"I would think so, Mitigomij. I see six canoes and probably eighteen to twenty warriors. They will not attack us on the river. They probably do not know how many warriors there are with us. They have seen all the canoes we have and are leery about an attack. My guess is that they will put a few scouts ashore and try to see what we have, and it is quite possible they will have already done that. When that happens, they will know that we do not have many warriors. Our women only carry knives and do not have the skills of a warrior. We will have to come up with a solid plan to rout this group. Our returning warriors are probably still at least a day away from meeting us. The rain, unlike us, wouldn't have slowed them down at all, but they won't be here to help with this problem."

We got into our canoes and started back to our group. When we arrived, we pulled along side Minowez-I and his son. Telling him what we had seen, we started to talk about a plan of defence.

"Our warriors are outnumbered two to one, but we might be able to have an element of surprise," I said.

"We'll have to split our meagre warrior group up. Minowez-I, I will leave two of my brothers, Kàg and

Wàgosh, with you and your son. With me I will have Mitigomij, the two warrior women, Makòns, and Miskwì. We will take two canoes, but the meat will have to be divided amongst the remainder, enabling us to travel more quickly. The enemy is at least a part of an afternoon behind us. They are coming slowly. I am sure their plans will be to attack us in the next morning or so. Try to push the people to hasten their speed."

"Mahingan, we'll be fine. Our warriors will soon be meeting us and we all will be safe. I will have Kàg lead the group and Nigig, Wàgosh, and I will guard the rear. Be careful, my friend. The Haudenosaunee are to be feared and not taken lightly."

"They have yet to meet us. It is the Algonquin that should be feared."

I hastily gathered my small force together. Because we did not have to go far from the river, I could take Mitigomij with us. He was by far the most fearsome warrior of our tribe and that big cat of his had proven his worth many times. The two young warriors still had a lot to learn, but their bravery was not in question. The women were to be feared. They fought as a team and were ruthless.

We travelled back down the river and put to shore before the bend. Pulling our canoes onto the shoreline, we hid them in the underbrush and then continued along the riverbank. When we reached the small bay that was nestled into the bend, we all decided that this was as good a spot as any for the trap. Figuring that the enemy would stay on this side of the river, we kept the bend between our group and theirs. I told everyone that we would wait to spring the ambush just as the Haudenosaunee were gliding into the bay, by staying concealed, they would not know how many of us there were. If we could kill or injure enough of them with our first couple of volleys, they might retreat downriver. This element of surprise along with the fear of not knowing our numbers might be enough to turn this skirmish to our advantage.

Silently, we waited in the cool afternoon shadows as their canoes glided silently into our range. Just as I was drawing my bow I heard a noise like a tree snapping in the cold. It was Mitigomij. He had fired his slingshot and caught a Haudenosaunee square in the face with a rock. The man screamed and fell back into the boat, sending the man behind him tumbling out into the bay. I heard one more crack of the slingshot before I could loosen my bow. I watched as the arrow struck a young warrior in the shoulder. Immediately, I restrung my bow and let loose another projectile. This one entered the eye of the man behind my first victim. By that time, as they were being showered with arrows from the shore, I could hear their screams of pain. Three of the canoes had retreated out of the bay as they had wounded and dying men in them. One of the remaining canoes was floating without any guidance, its occupants all dead.

However, we had a problem. Two canoes had landed and their occupants were intent on facing the hidden menace that had ambushed them. There were four of them, and they had the two young warriors cornered a distance from me. As I ran to their aid, I could see Makòns spurting blood from a neck wound and his assailant hitting him on the head with a war club. The two women were aiding Miskwì. Kìnà Odenan had her knife buried in the back of a Haudenosaunee. The man then screamed as Agwanìwon Ikwe hit the dying man with her war club full in the face. The warrior who had killed Makòns now had realized his worst nightmare. Makadewà Wàban. As the man turned to the sound of the panther's scream, the animal struck him full in the face. They rolled down the small embankment with the cat tearing chunks of flesh from his prey.

"Mitigomij, call the cat off. Let this man live to tell of his ordeal. We have vanquished them; the others are leaving in their canoe."

As they left, they reached into the bloody water and pulled the man out. Makadewà Wàban, standing up to his withers in the red water, screamed a bone-chilling warning to the men escaping. You could see the fear in their eyes as they hurried from the bloody waters.

We had won this small battle, but it had come at a terrible price. A young warrior. It was a great loss.

I knelt on the shore with Makòns in my arms and his blood on my soul. The lives of the Omàmiwinini people were always in the hands of Kitchi Manitou. Our lives seemed to be always a battle against starvation, grief, and the constant fear of our enemies. Nevertheless, we had to believe in our love of family to survive, or else all was in vain.

We put the body of Makòns into the canoe and caught up with our people. After learning of the young warrior's demise, the women started to sing a death song in his honour.

By the end of the day, we met with twenty of our warriors. The women and boys were elated to see them, and for me and the other warriors it was a great relief to know that we would have safety in numbers and added help when we had to portage. We were now able to lighten our loads, and with the extra labour we could arrive at our summer encampment in three days.

Makòns' family took his death hard. He was the eldest son and a good provider. Their cries of anguish were heard throughout the village. He had died a warrior and his story would be told around our fires for years to come.

The next few weeks were busy ones as our women prepared the pijakì meat for the winter and worked on the hides. Furthermore, in the next while, we would have many visitors.

21

THE PACT AND THE WARRIOR JOURNEY

AS THE WARM SUMMER days started to shorten, we decided that the twins Esiban and Agwingos would make the Wysoccan Journey to manhood together with the other boys in the village who were of age. Our people had used this rite as an entrance into manhood since time began. It was necessary if the young men wished to become warriors or leaders in our society. We selected only the strongest and healthiest boys to take the journey.

It was up to the Shaman of the village to administer the intoxicating medicine, wysoccan. The Shaman would dig up the root of the jimsonweed and make the wysoccan. He would then give the boys small doses until they became mad. The drug induced mental derangement and memory loss so they could enter manhood with no recollection of their childhood. This would continue for twenty days and then the dosage lessened. Before the dosage wore off completely, the Shaman brought them back to the village. Then they were observed to see if they had any memories of their former lives. If the boys showed signs of remembering, they were taken back and the rite continued.

The young boys that we selected for this, we took into the woods and put in wooden enclosures. This was to ensure that when they were in the deranged state of the medicine they would not wander off and cause themselves harm.

With their childhood memories now erased, instruction in the ways of becoming a warrior began. It was the duty of the elders to select the young boys for this journey. After the selection, the village hosted a night of feasting, drumming, and dancing in honour of those chosen.

That night our family unit gathered to celebrate the twins' selection for this honour. The women prepared a huge meal for the entire celebratory group. From sundown to daybreak, we danced, drummed, and told stories. This would be the last night that these young men would recognize their families. When they finished their Wysoccan Journey, they would have to be reintroduced to the people who were their family.

Esiban and Agwingos danced and ate the whole night without ever stopping to take a rest. Their mother stood and watched with tears in her eyes knowing that she was about to lose her beloved boys to warriorhood and that they would re-emerge from their journey without any remembrance of her.

The next morning we took all the boys to the woods. There we had prepared the wooden enclosures where they would spend the next twenty days. Inside each of the pens there was a robe to lie on. The Shaman gave them their first dosage of the medicine and the exhausted boys then went to sleep.

Only two men observed them while they were there: the Shaman and their guardian. They watched over the boys and supplied them with water. Mitigomij, who was the appointed guardian for the next twenty days, would never leave the area. The families took food and water and left it in a predetermined spot where Mitigomij went and picked it up every day. The food was for him and the Shaman, the water for the boys. All this time the Shaman increased the dosage of the medicine, causing the boys to hallucinate.

While all this went on, Mìgàdinàn-àndeg and his Nippissing warriors revisited us. They brought with them many of their elders, women, and children.

"Mìgàdinàn-àndeg," I said, "what has brought you and your people to our lands?"

"Mahingan, I have come to trade, feast, and talk of peace."

"Then, my friend, you are welcome. We will open our lodges for you to stay in while you visit. I'll send our young hunters out to bring back game for the grand feast that we will have."

For the next few days, we hunted and fished to prepare for the celebration. During this time, we also traded for the one thing that the Nippissing were known for, ozàwàbik (copper). The Nippissing lived in an area where it was easily found. Their Shamans made amulets out of the brown-coloured mineral that were highly valued by my people. Their people also made earrings, bracelets, and arrowheads from this precious gift from Kitchi Manitou.

However, for once we also had something that the Nippissing wanted, buffalo robes. They had never seen a robe this large and were willing to give us large amounts of copper for this animal's skin. The trading continued for three days and, in the end, everyone was happy with what had been obtained in the process.

After the trading was completed, it was decided that we would have games of skill, archery, running, slingshot, and spear competitions. The Nippissing knew that our most talented warrior in the weapons skills, Mitigomij, was busy with his duties as a guardian, so they felt quite confident in their chances. These war-rior games were a test of abilities and prestige between tribes. Each Nation selected warriors to go head to head in these competitions and the betting was heavy on all the individual participants.

Kàg, Wàgosh, and I decided that we would par-ticipate in the running competition. They knew that I was the fastest runner in our family unit. With this in mind, they would run with me and cause interference with the other runners, enabling me to get in the lead without being tripped or jostled. We would still have to find one or two more warriors to run with our team. Whenever we had running competitions, unless it was over short distances, it was a no-holds-barred event as far as interfering with the runners. This helped in our training of being a warrior because in times of battle when you were running among the enemy, they would not let you pass them without trying to strike or knock you down. Survival of the fittest at all times.

The running competition was always the final event to be contested when we had games. As the games proceeded, it was evident that the two Nations were evenly matched, with neither group gaining an edge over the other. People who were betting on the outcomes were losing on one match and then winning on the next. All the participants and onlookers were having a good time with a great deal of laughter and many friendships being made.

After four days, the running contest was set to start. Elders from both camps had gone out together on the previous days and blazed a trail through the woods that the contestants had to follow. That day the elders took people from all the Nippissing and Algonquin camps and situated them as spectators and guides so no one would run off course. The runners were allowed no weapons, except for one small stick. You could strike a runner with this stick below the shoulders as a way of letting them know that you were approaching him and wanted to pass, or to keep him from passing. If struck with this switch, it would sting and bring a welt up on your skin, but it taught you to be vigilant, because if you were in battle and did not know where your enemy was it could cost you your life.

"Mahingan, we have found two more runners to be with us," said Kàg.

"Who are they?" I asked.

"Don't worry, brother. You will know in good time and be pleased with their inclusion," answered Wàgosh.

That next morning the race was to begin. Consequently, that night there was a lot of bragging and betting going on. The competitor who won the race would be showered with gifts from the people that had placed bets on them. Everyone was in a celebratory mood, feasting, dancing, and telling stories throughout the night.

After awhile I began to feel tired and decided that it would be a wise decision to obtain a good night's sleep. With Ishkodewan at my side, I went and found Wàbananang and the three of us retired in our lodge for the night. As I lay beside my wife, I placed my ear upon her stomach to see if there was any sound from our child. Singing a song to him, it was not long before I was dreaming of my ancestors.

My brothers and the two people they had recruited to run with us woke me in the morning.

"Agwanìwon Ikwe and Kìnà Odenan, I am honoured to have both of you run with me."

"Mahingan, we want to be on the winning side so we had no choice but to side with you," said a laughing Kìnà Odenan.

"We also knew that you would share any of your winning gifts with us," said Agwanìwon Ikwe with a smile on her face.

"Kìnà Odenan and Agwanìwon Ikwe, maybe no one will bet on me, and then if I did win there would not be any spoils to share."

With that, we all laughed and proceeded to have something to eat with all of the other participants. There had been heavy dew that night and this would make the footing slippery in spots, but it all added to the excitement and challenge.

The course would take the morning to run. The elders would make sure it was a difficult challenge. I looked around and counted over a hundred runners. With this many competitors it would be important to keep the leaders in view at all times. For that reason it was very essential that our team keep together for as long as possible and run good interference for me.

After the meal the contestants started to drift to the starting place. It was not long before the elders started to call everyone to the line with the drums. Once we approached the starting line, we were told that the drummers would stop drumming. Upon the instruction of the elders, they would commence again, and that was our signal to start. They would not quit drumming until a winner crossed the finish line.

While all the trading and athletic contests were happening, our young boys were continuing on their journey to manhood under the watchful eyes of the Shaman and Mitigomij.

Mitigomij had always been very protective of the young men who were taking the journey here in the woods. He had taught these boys the skills needed to hunt and fish and now they were being administered the wysoccan medicine so that they would forget all of their childhood. It then would be up to him and the other warriors to introduce them into warriorhood and help renew their skills. They would also have to help them reacquaint with their families, but to never tell them about their childhood. These young boys had to be trained in the art of being a warrior. It was important to the survival of the Algonquin Nation that it always had strong and skilled young men to replace the men lost in battle and other misfortunes.

During the several days that Mitigomij had been with the Shaman and the boys, he had watched them become increasingly delirious. He also observed as they cried out in pain and then turned violent, grabbing the wooden enclosure they were in, shaking it and trying to escape. When the warriors made these wysoccan enclosures, they took great pains in ensuring that they would withstand all attempts of escape by the young men. It would be a handful if one of them ever got out and Mitigomij would have to capture him and put the deranged boy back again. No one had ever escaped an appointed guardian yet, and he was making sure that it would not happen to him. Whenever a boy was sleeping, Mitigomij would always check the enclosure to make sure there was no broken rope or weakening wooden supports. He would also put water into the cage while the boys slept. The less human contact they had the better.

The Shaman administered the medicine in increased dosages until they were very mad. He then started to decrease the medicine until they were still in a delirium state. When they reached this level, they were then taken back to the village.

Mitigomij and the Shaman had been with the boys for fourteen days. The time was ending. Would they be successful with their endeavour? Alternatively, would they have to repeat this with any of the young men? The next six days would tell the tale. Would the Pact be sealed between the Wysoccan Journey and Warriorhood?

During one of the visits by the village women bringing food and water, he was told that the Nippissing had arrived to the land of the Omàmiwinini. Trading and warrior games were taking place. Mitigomij was disappointed that he was missing all this, but what he was doing held much more importance for the future of his people than a few trade items and games.

As the runners all stood around the starting point, there was a lot of bravado taking place. One tall Nippissing warrior approached me and said, "I am Ojàwashkwà Animosh (Blue Dog)."

"I am very honoured to meet you," I replied.

"They tell me, Mahingan, that you are the swiftest warrior of the Omàmiwinini."

"Well, Ojàwashkwà Animosh, if I have to tell you how good I am then I am not that good. You'll have to find out today if what they say is true."

"Spoken like a true warrior, my friend. You will let your actions speak to your reputation. I will take that into consideration. Until we meet at the end, good luck and I know that if I can beat you I will have won a great victory!"

No sooner had our conversation ended than the elders gave the signal for the drummers to begin. With one large whoop that left the surrounding forest in a continuous echo, the runners lunged toward the trail with everyone jostling for their spot in the mass. You could hear the snapping of the sticks on nearby bodies and the yelling of the warriors. It sounded like a pitch battle, but without the bloodshed.

I led my co-runners to the left side of this howling pack and tried to gain an open spot to run unhindered, but we were fast approaching the forest and here the trail narrowed with a collision of bodies. With me in the lead, my group and I weaved around a few runners to gain an advantage to the trail. On my left ran Wàgosh and on my right was Kàg. Directly behind me were the two women. I had strained to reach the trail ahead of a group of about fifteen runners who were clumped together and having a grand time hitting each other with their switches. Ahead of my group about seven or eight paces were about ten runners. They were not the leaders, but they were keeping pace with the groups that were setting the pace.

We hit the opening of the pine forest just ahead of the two groups that were going at each other with their switches. I could hear the two women behind me screaming and using their sticks on a few men who had approached too closely. Just as we arrived, off to my right rear, I could see a crash of bodies that were colliding in one huge ball of humanity. They fell, taking with them a few other participants in the tangle of legs and arms.

Now that we were into the deep woods, the morning sun had not dried out the dew and our footing was very precarious. Twice, a group had tried to gain on us but the lead runner had slipped on a wet rock or a downed tree limb and tumbled, taking with him a few of the runners who were following.

My group was having no problem for the time being keeping up with the runners ahead of us. We were slowly increasing the distance on the rivals following us. No one was foolish enough to try to pass in the narrow confines of the woods. Everyone was waiting for their chance that they knew would come on the route ahead.

The people that were standing along the trail to prevent the runners from straying cheered everyone on. Once the field passed, they would work their way to another vantage point that they knew of or they would go back to the village and wait for the finish. The forest run was a flat terrain, but I figured that in the next little while things would change. My accompanying friends were showing no sign of strain from the pace that had been set. They were continually singing and talking to keep their morale up.

When we left the canopy of the forest, we entered an area of waist-high grass. This part of the trail led us to a huge rock climb that took us along a rocky ridge. Here our stamina received a test as we ran and climbed up the rock. Because of the width of the face of the rocky incline, there was lots of room to pass anyone ahead of you. Again the sound of the small switches was heard striking runners ahead and behind.

Wàgosh and the women were preoccupied with several runners who were making a move on my left, while Kàg and I were hastily trying to catch a group ahead of us. They were bent over, scaling the rock and running on all fours. This gave us a chance to whip their legs with our switches. After hitting them numerous times, the stinging of their legs slowed them down and Kàg and I were able to hurry past. They had not been able to strike back at us because of the positions they were in while scaling this escarpment. As we passed, they tried to take a couple of swings at us, but it did not hinder either one of us in the least.

I reached the top, my lungs burning and my legs aching from the climb. However, upon looking down, I saw all the remaining warriors in various positions of scaling this obstacle and I knew there was no time to waste. Gulping as much air as I could into my lungs I continued. After about five or six running lengths all of my guardians joined me and I gained a sense of relief knowing we were still all together.

Running along the ridge, we were able see what the terrain ahead looked like and how many competitors there were. We were able to see about five separate groups ahead and they were all keeping a torrid pace.

As we started the incline down the escarpment, it enabled us to see the leader. With a smile, I recognized the warrior that we were chasing. Ojàwashkwà Animosh! Now the race was really on!

As we left the ridge, we came upon a small stream. Because of the thickness of the surrounding forest, we had to run in the stream with water that came up to around our ankles. This slowed everyone down and enabled us to catch up to the group ahead. In the ensuing melee of splashing water, whooping, and sticks whacked against bare skin, my group passed the runners ahead when their leader slipped in the riverbed and fell with some of his followers tumbling onto him. It was also not without the loss of one of our people; Agwanìwon Ikwe also went down with a splash. Part of being a running guardian is that if you fall the others do not go back for you. The object is to always protect the lead runner and put all other feelings aside, not unlike battle where if you have to rescue one person at the risk of putting the rest of your fellow warriors in peril it is not worth the risk.

Leaving the embankment of the stream, we were able to pass one other group who were caught up in the mud and water. Now there were only three groups left ahead of us and we had them in sight. The race had now taken up over half the morning. Time and distance was running out and we would have to start to make our final moves and quickly.

When we vacated the embankment, we had to cross a small meadow before we reached the forest again for the return trip. The grass was waist-high and this gave us a tremendous opportunity. I looked at my companions and gave a nod. With that, we ran as fast as we could, skirting to the right of the group ahead of us. We were past them before they knew it. They had been content to take their time through the open field. We ran, jumped, and leaped through the entanglement of grass and small bushes, catching them completely unaware. Not one person was struck with a switch in this encounter, and as we entered the forest the last two groups were in sight.

If we were going to win this race, it would have to be here in the forest before we hit the last clearing that would take us to the village and finish line. As we ran, we laid out our plan to take over the lead. Ojàwashkwà Animosh and his remaining two guardians were just behind a group of young Algonquin warriors from our deceased brother-in-law, Makwa's Omàmiwinini tribe, the Sàginitaouigama. These young warriors were setting a torrid pace and it would take a lot of skill to catch them. Our plan was to stay on the heels of Ojàwashkwà Animosh and his group until they made their move. At that time, we would set our plan in place.

I looked around at my companions. Everyone was covered in sweat and mud. All of us had large welts on our bodies from where the switches had hit us. We were also bleeding from encounters with tree limbs and rocks, but we all had smiles on our faces.

We were close to where we thought Ojàwashkwà Animosh would make his move, when to our surprise the group that we had passed in the long grass caught up to all of us and made their attempt to pass the group. Then in the next few minutes, all that we could hear was yelling and the sound of switches hitting bare skin. After being struck several times with switches, my skin started to feel like it was on fire. Then, at that precise moment, Kàg's experience shone through. On the narrow trail where barely two people could run side by side he made a decision that would spring us free from the trailing group. Kàg turned and dropped his shoulder into the lead runner, knocking him down. He then stuck his leg out and tripped the next runner and in the melee that followed everyone behind us was yelling, shouting, and falling in a large mass of bodies. This enabled me, Wàgosh, and Kìnà Odenan to pull away from the trailing group and concentrate on what was ahead of us.

Ojàwashkwà Animosh now took advantage of the distraction that was happening behind him and the leaders. The young warriors in the lead broke stride just a bit to see what all the noise was about to their rear. This was all the opening that the Nippissing warrior and his group needed. They lunged forward into the leaders, knocking the two trailing warriors off the trail and laid their switches onto the remainder of the group. Before the leaders knew it, the Nippissing warriors were past them, and we were right on their heels. The young warriors who had been leading were dumbfounded that two groups had passed them in such a flurry of activity. Even more surprised was Ojàwashkwà Animosh when he realized that we were hot on his trail.

As we left the forest, we could now hear the drummers. All that remained was crossing a small stream and scaling an embankment about the height of two men. This was where we would make our move.

The Nippissing were now equal in numbers to us: three warriors. The six of us splashed through the water and arrived simultaneously at the embankment. Wàgosh and Kìnà Odenan arrived just ahead of me and they joined their hands together. I jumped onto their clasped hands and all in one movement they tossed me as hard as they could upwards. They threw me so hard that I felt like I was flying like a kiniw. Rolling as I hit the ground above the embankment, I came to an upright position and immediately started running.

I could see the village and hear the cheering of the people as well as the drummers and their chants. My legs and lungs felt like they were going to burn from the inside out. I took a quick glance behind and caught a glimpse of a rapidly approaching Ojàwashkwà Animosh. Seeing him gave me a huge burst of final energy. The only noise that I could hear was the pounding of my odey (heart) and my feet. Everything else was blocked out. My body felt like it was a feather floating in the air, no longer feeling any pain, only a sense of oneness with the earth. Sweat was pouring off my forehead and I had to keep wiping it away as it was stinging my eyes and obscuring my vision. Then it was all over. The dreamlike world vanished and I could hear the whooping of the people in the village and the sudden halt of the drums. Did I win or is this all a dream? Then people started singing my name and patting me on the back.

I was exhausted. I felt someone grab me in a bear hug and say, "Mahingan you are a great adversary." It was Ojàwashkwà Animosh.

When he released me, I collapsed into an exhausted heap. I then felt a soft hand on my cheek. It was my dear wife; she had put a vessel of water to my lips and simultaneously kissed me gently on the forehead.

"I love you, Mahingan, my wonderful husband," she said.

With those words, I felt my whole body overcome with a tingling sensation and sudden warmth. I have never cared for someone as much as I cared for my loving Wàbananang. I would be lost emotionally without her.

That night as we feasted, I told the story of my victory and then all the competitors in turn told in detail how I had defeated them. For two more days, the celebrations went on. Then at the end of the second day, Mìgàdinànàndeg rose and spoke.

"For many years our people have battled each other and a common foe, the Haudenosaunee. My people and I have now decided that we will accept your offer of the mìkisesimik, signifying peace between us. Mahingan, now I in return present you with our mìkisesimik to seal the pact."

Rising, I took the belt from the Nippissing chief to the thundering yells and whoops of all in attendance.

"Mìgàdinàn-àndeg, we are now allies and will remain as such until the end of time. We will defend each other in times of war and provide the other aid in times of famine. The Omàmiwinini and Nippissing are now brothers!"

With that, our drummers and singers started to play and chant and the people from our two Nations began to dance and celebrate. It was the ending of a great day.

The next morning as the Nippissing started to break camp to leave, our attentions diverted to the sound of the Shaman announcing his return. All eyes turned in his direction and to those that were following him. We could see Mitigomij and the young men who had taken the Wysoccan Journey. The boys stood at the edge of the village with a stunned expression on their faces. They did not recognize anyone or their surroundings. Their child-hood journey was finished. Now they were ready to begin the warrior path and to all that it led.

22

PREPARING
FOR THE WINTER

THAT FALL OUR FAMILY group left the summer village and travelled just north of the big island in the Kitcisìpi Sìbì. With the buffalo meat that we had preserved from the hunt, our bellies would not shrink like the previous winter. The women and children had been able to forage and find a good supply of roots and berries to store for the winter season. Mitigomij had taken upon himself the responsibility of teaching the twins their warrior skills. The three of them were very proficient and had been able to supply the camp with a good supply of game, and with the success of the other hunters in our village, we were able to set aside a good supply of venison and fish.

The two warrior women had decided that they would spend the winter with us, definitely a welcome addition as warriors and hunters. Agwaniwon Ikwe and Kìnà Odenan built their own lodge for the winter months and set about helping the elders gather their food for the winter. These women were two of the most ruthless warriors there was when it came to a battle, but they had an immense soft spot for elders and children. They could always be depended on to aid the villagers who could not keep up their supply of food because of age or sickness. Whenever people saw them walking in the vicinity they were always feted and could not pass a family's home without someone inviting them in for a meal or just to share cedar tea with them. All the people loved and admired these women.

Both women were born to families that had no sons, and so at an early age they became attached to each other like siblings. They showed an immense sense of charity to all the people around them and were never afraid to help friends and family in times of need. As they grew older a man called Kànikwe (No Hair) took it upon himself to teach them how to hunt and fish. Kànikwe had realized that because these girls came from families of no brothers, there would be problems when their parents grew older and could not hunt and gather for themselves. Furthermore, Kànikwe owed his life to these two young girls at the time.

Kànikwe had gotten his name when he was a young warrior. In a battle with the Haudenosaunee who had raided his village, two of the enemy had overpowered him. As one of them held him, the other took his scalp. Kànikwe, though in immense pain and bloodied, was able to take his knife and bury it in the groin of the man taking his scalp. As the enemy screamed in pain, the other man who was holding him loosened his grip for a moment. This was all the opportunity that Kànikwe needed. With an upward motion, he drove his knife into the man's lower jaw. Bathed in blood and sweat and grasping his war club, he finished killing both of the men. Kànikwe grabbed his scalp from the bloody hands of the dead man, who had only minutes before held his life in the balance.

Kànikwe was quick to realize that without doing anything with his wound he would die within days. Leaving the battle between the two antagonistic foes, he rushed into the pine forest where he knew there was a beehive. Wiping the blood from his eyes, he climbed the tree where the bees had made their home. Impervious to the stings of the bees he reached into the tree trunk where the bees had their hive. Grabbing gobs of honey, he smeared it on his hairless and bloodied head and swollen, bee-stung face. Covered in the gooey mess of honey and blood he slid down the tree and ran from the furious bees to a marsh. There he passed out in the mud from the pain of the bee stings and his head wound. There the young girls Agwanìwon Ikwe and Kìnà Odenan found him hours after the battle. They then took him back to their village where they fed him and helped with his healing.

Kànikwe became devoted to these young women from that moment on and grew to be their protector and teacher. His scalp healed, but it never grew hair again and he always painted his head black with a red line down the middle. He then took the scalp he had wrestled out of the Haudenosaunee warrior's dying hands and tied it to the handle of his own war club.

Through the years after the two women's parents died, they wandered among the Omàmiwinini tribes offering their warrior and hunting skills. They were always welcome and were inseparable. Their friend and protector Kànikwe became a recluse among his people. In later years he enjoyed being alone. Every once in a while he would wander into one of the Omàmiwinini camps and would stay until he decided to move on, but wherever he stayed he always helped supply game for the village and provided any other skills that were needed. No one had seen him for the last couple of winters and thought he either had taken up with the Huron or had passed away to the Creator.

The fall soon stretched on with warm days, cool nights, and heavy frosts in the morning. The animals that slept for the winter had started to disappear from the forest. On one of these sunny days Kàg, Mitigomij, and I were hunting along the river. We had not been out very long before we caught the scent of a shigàg and the sound of a person singing a song of thanks to Kitchi Manitou. Not knowing what lay ahead, we entered the heavy underbrush to the side of the game trail we had been on, to see who would appear. As the voice grew nearer so did the smell of the skunk. The three of us looked at each other in bewilderment. Were the spirits playing tricks on us? We could smell a skunk and hear a song of praise. Then to our amazement, we saw what was causing all the noise and smell. Out of the cover of the birch forest that enclosed our trail walked a very large and smelly man.

I immediately recognized him.

"Kànikwe, have you been wrestling with a skunk?"

"Oh, Mahingan," he replied, "my friend shigàg had led me to a honey hive and did not want to share. We then had a disagreement about who would get what. He did not take kindly to me poking him with my spear and then lifting him on his underbelly and tossing him aside. I wasn't greedy, I only took the honey and he still has his bees to eat when he regains his composure."

"Well, our friend," said Kàg, "you will walk behind us. I think that the only people in our village who will help you at this moment are Agwanìwon Ikwe and Kìnà Odenan."

When Kàg mentioned the names of the two women, you could see the eyes of Kànikwe light up. When we got back to the village, the people knew we were coming long before they heard or saw us. The smell was that bad.

The two laughing women grabbed Kànikwe and covered him with ashes and charcoal from the fire pits. This would mask the smell until such time that it disappeared from his body.

Luckily for Kànikwe, he had suffered no bee stings because he had dulled their senses with smoke. He never took all the honey from any of the hives that he raided. He always left enough for the bees to survive. It was because of their honey that he was able to live after suffering the horrendous scalping.

The days after Kànikwe arrived were spent harvesting manòmin (rice) on a lake that was half a day's walk from our village. Not wanting to carry our canoes that far through the forest, we made what we needed when we arrived. Half the village came with us to help with the harvesting and preparation of the rice. The wild rice was a food that was essential to our survival over the winter. When available our women used it in all their cooking.

After building the canoes, we were ready to start the harvesting of the rice. Each canoe had two people in it: one person who was responsible for moving the canoe through the rice bed while the other bent the stems over into the boat, knocking the rice off the stalks. The person who did the knocking held a stick in each hand. They used one stick to bend the rice stalk into the boat and the other to knock off the rice heads. The harvesters always made sure that enough rice seed ended up in the water to reseed the beds, ensuring that there would be enough to harvest the following fall. While we were harvesting the rice, we were also able to hunt the thousands of geese and ducks that also were taking advantage of this easily accessible food.

When the people had harvested all the rice for the village needs, we then had to prepare it. We dried the heads by spreading it out on birch bark, but first the women had to trample it on mats to break off the long, sharp beards. As the grains lay drying on birch bark mats, the people continually moved it with sticks to allow the air and sun to do their work; this took a couple of days to accomplish. Once all the rice dried, the hulls started to crack open. The people finished cracking open the hulls by digging shallow pits and then lining it with skins. The men then danced on the seed, singing the manòmin harvest song.

The people then put what they had cracked on birch bark trays and tossed it in the air, letting the wind carry away the chaff. After washing the rice, we placed it in bark boxes and bags of skin.

With the harvest finished, we had a feast of thanksgiving. On the way home we took our time and collected as many acorns as we could carry. When we arrived in the village, the women took the acorns and the baskets they were in and placed them in the stream that ran beside our camp. Here they would soak the nuts for two or three days, making them easy to crack open and enabling the women to obtain the meat in the shell. The shells would then be dried and burnt in our fires.

That winter would be one of our better winters in a long time. No one starved because we had lots of meat, and our supplies of rice, acorns, and berries were abundant. A significant problem during the winter was to contend with the congestion in our lungs caused by the smoke in the lodges. Our fires were continually burning to keep us warm and to cook our meals. Even though the days were cold, we tried to spend as much time outside as we could to keep our lungs clear.

During that time of the year, the women made clothes out of the hides from the game that the men had hunted all summer. The men meanwhile spent the winter months hunting when the weather was favourable, making new weapons and repairing the ones we had.

Because of the abundance of food that winter, it made it easier for the pregnant women in our village to stay healthy. My wife Wàbananang was expecting during the

Onàbanad Tibik-kìzis (Crust Moon, March). This was the moon when the snow was crusty and we could walk on it without our snowshoes most days.

When a child was born into our tribe, it was the beginning of the cycle of life. He or she would have much to learn and many ceremonies to proceed through until reaching the end of the journey, death.

Wàbananang selected the woman that she wanted to be her midwife. She was an elder who through the years had delivered many babies and never had lost a mother or child. This was almost unheard of among our people, because there were many times that either the mothers or the child died during childbirth. Kìjekwe (Honoured Woman) always knew what herbs and teas to use to help end the pregnancy. For the last several weeks of my wife's pregnancy, she had given her lots of miskominag anìbìsh (raspberry leaf tea). When my wife's time drew near, Kìjekwe prepared a place for her in her lodge. There she would look after her until the child was born. Then I would be sent for if all went well.

As a man, I was not allowed into the birthing lodge, so I asked my brothers if they wanted to go on a hunt for a few days. Kàg and Mitigomij said that they would accompany me. Wàgosh, who was still practically a newlywed even though he had got married in the spring, said he would stay back and watch over the village. The three of us laughed at this because we knew that it was not the village that he wanted to watch over. Kàg's twin sons, who had taken their manhood journey that summer, decided that they would come on the hunt with us. The two young warriors had not yet earned or been given adult names, so we still called them by their childhood names.

With the small dog and Ishkodewan leading the way and Mitigomij's black panther trailing in the woods, we started out on our hunt. The decision had been made that we would only go out for two days, travelling as far as we could the first day and then returning by a different route the second. Everyone except Mitigomij pulled a toboggan in case we were successful on our hunt.

"Mahingan, do you think that Wàbananang will bring you a man child to spread your seed for years to come?" asked my brother Kàg.

"Kàg you know as well as I do that decision is made by Kitchi Manitou. All children when they are born to us already have their lives planned out by the Creator Force. How they follow that trail is in their own hands and if it is the wrong one, he or she will be given a sign to redirect them back down the pre-chosen path."

"My brother, I had a dream that you would have a son," said Mitigomij.

"Ah, that would please me! A son strengthens the Algonquin Nation. They can't bear children like a daughter can, nevertheless they grow up to hunt and defend their people."

Before we could continue our conversation, the small dog and Ishkodewan started to whimper.

"Esiban and Agwingos, the animals have caught the scent of something. Be ready to keep up to them," I said. "Go," I said to the two whimpering animals. On my command, they went with the speed of a shot arrow. The sound of the dog barking and the wolf howling made for an odd reverberation in the forest. They headed toward a part of the forest that was mostly tall pines, with the twins running to keep up with them.

Having Mitigomij with us slowed Kàg and me down. We did not want to set a pace that would cause him to fall back of us. It was not long before we could hear that the dog and wolf had something cornered. Then we heard the unmistakable roar of a makwa. I could feel my heart quicken knowing that the animals and the two young men were coming onto a very irritable and hungry animal that probably had just awakened from a long sleep.

"Kàg and Mahingan, you must leave me and rush to the hunt. The bear will be a handful for the small dog, Ishkodewan, and the twins. Makadewà Wàban and I will be there before you know it. They need your help!"

Kàg and I then broke into a run. The crust on the snow made for easy footing and helped to speed up our arrival. As we ran, we could hear the sounds of the three animals and the yelling of the twins. With the cold crisp air and the stillness of the pinewoods, the sound of the ensuing battle between men and animals echoed through the forest. When we arrived, we could not believe our eyes! There was one huge bear backed up against a deadfall with a snarling dog and wolf attacking him from different sides and the twins shooting arrows at the animal. The bear had six arrows stuck into his throat but he was still bravely fighting on. Every time he roared, blood from his wounds sprayed onto his attackers. Both the dog and wolf had bloodied muzzles from their continued attacks on the bear's withers. When the big boar saw us, he raised himself up on his hind legs and let loose a roar that sent shivers up my spine and echoed throughout the pine forest, reminiscent to the roar of a waterfall. At that instant, the twins let loose another two arrows. Both of the projectiles struck the bear in his heart, and with one last bellow, he dropped like a large tree crashing in the forest. After he hit the ground, his body twitched a couple of times and then a big gush of air emitted from the carcass. The dog and wolf went up to the bear and sniffed it cautiously. The twins seemed caught up in a sense of disbelief for a few moments, and then they raised their bows in the air and whooped. After that, they started singing a song of thanksgiving to Kitchi Manitou and the spirit of the bear. The song thanked the bear for the brave battle and Kitchi Manitou for protecting them during the clash. I walked up to the boys and handed them some tobacco to make an offering to the Creator.

Kàg then said to Esiban and Agwingos, "Sons, this is your first kill. Your uncles and I will help you take the meat and hide back to the village. However, you are responsible for the butchering. Do not forget the dog and wolf. They deserve some choice meat for their part in this hunt."

As the boys started their job, Mitigomij arrived on the scene with a big smile; we could see the pride in his eyes. Kàg and I both knew that these young men had been taught well by their uncle since their entrance into manhood.

While the boys worked away at their task, Kàg and I gathered wood and cedar boughs for a fire and shelter. Mitigomij busied himself with cooking our bear meat meal.

As darkness approached, the twins finished cutting up the bear. They approached the fire and we asked them to tell their story of the successful hunt. After they told their story, Mitigomij stood up to speak.

"Esiban and Agwingos," Mitigomij said, "I have decided on your new names."

Because Mitigomij was their uncle protector and teacher, he was entitled to give them their warrior names.

Mitigomij said, "As I watched your successful hunt, I was reminded of another great warrior, your uncle, Makwa. He fought and killed a bear and wore the scars for the rest of his life. I know that he was watching over the two of you during your hunt today. With this in mind, Esiban and Agwingos, both of you will carry the name of your uncle and this powerful beast from the forest. Esiban, from this day forward your name will be Makwa and Agwingos you will be known as Wàbek. Both names mean bear in our language. The two of you have earned it and your dead uncle and the bear will be your spirit protectors."

Kàg and I then stood and sang their names and told the story of how they earned them.

That night as I lay in the shelter I thought of my wife and the birth of my child. I hoped that if it were a boy that Mitigomij would be still on this earth to teach him the ways of our people when the time came.

The next morning we loaded all the bear meat and the hide on the toboggans for the journey home.

❋ ❋ ❋

"Your time is coming, Wàbananang. The water in your womb has broken and the child will soon be here," said Kìjekwe.

"I can feel the child move; it wants to come into our world. The pain is starting to be more intense," answered Wàbananang.

"Here, take more tea. It will help you with the pain."

Kìjekwe now started to massage Wàbananang, burn sweet grass, and sing the birthing song. Outside the wàginogàn, the Shaman and other women started to sing. This continued well into the night. Then near the coming of daylight, the sound of a small child crying told all the people outside that the baby had entered the world of Turtle Island.

Inside, Kìjekwe held up the baby in the light of the fire to show the mother her new son. She then went to a corner of the lodge where there was a bag filled with milkweed and cattail down. With this, she made a diaper for the new son of Mahingan. Then she wrapped him in a specially made hide that had been decorated with symbols to protect the child. As she lay the boy down near the fire to wrap him into the hide she noticed that he had two marks, one on the nape of his neck and the other on his right rump. She thought to herself this was a good sign; the Creator had marked him for greatness so that he could find him whenever there was a need to carry out the work of Kitchi Manitou. Just before Kìjekwe wrapped him up to give to his mother, she took a small medicine bag that she had made and into it she put the umbilical cord that she had cut off the boy's belly.

Putting the bag around his neck she said, "This was your attachment to your mother, keeping you alive while you were in her womb. For the rest of your life it will be in your medicine bag, keeping the attachment even after your journey into the warrior world."

My son was born the night after the twins had made their kill. When we entered the village just before dark the next day, Wàgosh came out to meet us.

"Brother, you have a son. Mother and child are healthy and waiting for you. The news gets even better, Mahingan. The Creator has marked him. He has the signs of a great warrior!"

I had a sudden rush of exhilaration. I sped to the midwife's lodge to see my wife and son. When I entered, I could see the two of them by the fire. He was suckling from his mother. She looked up at me and smiled, handing me my son. When I picked him up, I could smell his mother's milk on his breath. He had lots of hair and a smile on his face; I pulled down the hide and found the marks from the Creator. This made me very happy. When I thought back to the past few days I immediately knew what his childhood name would be. I took it as a sign from the Creator that because he was born while we were on a hunt, that he should be named in that honour. When I told Wàbananang his name and why I chose it, her face lit up.

"Mahingan, Anokì (Hunt) is a wonderful name. The events that led up to you picking the name are good signs, he will make you proud."

Little did I know that the not-so-distant future would be one of danger for my family, my village, and me.

23

RED SKIES

WITH LOTS TO EAT and the birth of five children that winter, our village was a very joyful place. Moreover, with the addition of the two warrior women and their friend Kìjekwe, plus the maturing of the twins, our small band gained needed warrior strength for the immediate future. Because Kìjekwe and the warrior women had no immediate family to provide for, they could provide lots of fresh meat for the elders and for the family of Makòns, who had died at the Battle of The Small Bay while we were returning from the buffalo hunt.

With all the snow melting in the forest and clearings, it turned the grass green and brought out the wildflowers. However, later in the spring there was a lack of rainfall, causing all the fauna to thirst for moisture.

This lack of water did not affect our people as much as the plant life, because we had access to the big river. By late spring, the weather had turned hotter than normal and the ground beneath our feet started to wither and go dormant. Subsequently, the lack of moisture was causing concern with the women, as they were finding the early summer roots that they collected were becoming sparse, and what they did find was of poor quality. Our hunters were also finding that the game was starting to move away from the area because the grass they fed on was dying off. We could feed ourselves with the ample fish and wildfowl from the river, but without the presence of large game, we would soon have to move our camp and follow their lead. This would affect our summer gathering with the other family units of our close Omàmiwinini brethren. We would have to move downriver and this would put us near the Haudenosaunee and danger.

As our days moved from the Wàbigon Tibik-kìzis (Flower Moon, May) into the Odeyimin Tibik-kìzis (Strawberry Moon, June), we could see the wildflowers start to die out from the lack of moisture. The absence of rain also prevented the wild strawberries in the meadows from growing to their usual size and flavour, stunting their growth.

The village now had to be overly vigilant with the cooking fires. The surrounding pine and birch forest was tinder dry, and it would not take much for a fire to start. The men started to take turns going to the high rocks that surrounded the village to keep watch in case of a fire. We brought all our canoes to the river and readied them in case we did have to abandon our campsite.

Nokomis's bosom feeds all the plants, animals, and men, but when she decides there has to be a renewal and rebirth she will use fire to do so.

Early into the Strawberry Moon, the air became very humid and heavy. Our people knew this was a sign from Nokomis that the rains would begin, but with the rains, she would also bring the fire from the sky, wàwàsamòg (lightning).

The third night after Nokomis's sign, the lightning lit up the skies for the whole evening, but there was no rain. Again, the next night the lightning came, and it was close enough to illuminate the river and the forests around us. Always the onimikì (thunder) accompanied the lightning, like huge drums in the sky, and on the second night it was so loud that we thought it was going to come out of the skies and devour us with its roar.

"Mahingan," said Mitigomij, "I had a dream last night that the fire would come soon. We must be prepared, for I fear that it will devour us if we are not ready. In my dream, we went to the small island that is sheltered by the big island where the rapids are fierce. This place will protect us, and in turn we will protect the island."

"Yes, Mitigomij. I know the place. Upriver from where we are and a day's travel by the river. The island has rapids to protect us from the north, with lots of game on the larger island, and we would be close to the mainland, which would enable us to hunt there also. We will prepare in the morning to go."

For the last two days during the thunder and lightning, our dogs had been cowering in our lodges. My wolf Ishkodewan, who was now full-grown, would not leave my side. In the evening, he crawled into our shelter, lies beside me, and whimpered throughout the night while we tried to sleep. The only one of our family who was not bothered by all the noise was Anokì. He slept through it all. Even Mitigomij's panther, Makadewà Wàban, was showing himself on the edge of the forest. The animals were warning us.

About an hour before dawn Kànikwe, Miskwì, and one of the twins, Wàbek, awakened the village.

They were yelling, "It has started, we can see the fire coming through the big pine forest to the north of us. We have to go."

"Kànikwe, how much time do we have?" Kàg asked.

"Until a bit after dawn," he replied.

By then the whole village was awake and we were grabbing all that we could carry. We totalled seventy-three people, of which twenty-two were warriors.

There was only enough time to make two trips to the canoes, but because of the limitations of the elders, we asked them to make only one trip.

I spoke to the warriors and told them that on the first trip we had to take all our weapons and hides. The women, elders, and older children would be responsible for the food stores. The younger children were to handle the dogs and watch over them. When we returned, we would load up the toboggans with everything else: our snowshoes, clothes, cooking utensils, and containers. The path through the pines to the canoes was well worn and one man could pull the toboggans. The rest of the warriors, women, and older children would carry all they could. There were some travois in the village that in the past we had used to bring in game. We had forty-two canoes, and we would fill them with all that they could carry. We would lash some of the canoes together because of the lack of paddlers.

By dawn the animals that were fleeing the onslaught of the fire were starting to run through the village. Our nostrils were filling with the smell of the burning forest, and we could hear the trees popping from the ferocity of the flames. Looking up, all we could see was a red sky to the north, floating embers, and ash.

"We must go now," I yelled to everyone. "Nokomis is sending her fire, and she will not spare us if we do not heed her warnings!"

With the sound of the forest crackling from the fire behind us, the people started toward the river and safety. Embers were flying through the air toward our village.

As we proceeded toward the river, we happened upon the predators of the forest that were patrolling the fire's perimeter. In the skies, the hawks were circling and along with the wolves, mink, pijiw (lynx), fox, and cougars, they were all feasting on the kinebik (snakes), wàbòz, and nanapàdjinikesì (mice) as they fled from the fire.

Making sure there was no one left behind was the responsibility of the older boys; they took one last patrol of the shoreline. By the time they finished their search, all the boats had been loaded and we shoved off into the river.

My canoe held my wife, son, Ishokodewan, and the small dog. The boat next to me carried Mitigomij, Wàbek, my brother's panther Makadewà Wàban, and a small boy who was sound asleep lying up against the big cat. Kàg and Wàgosh were close by in their boats with their wives and the other twin Makwa.

As we started to paddle upstream to the island, we made it a point to help any distressed animals that were in the river. The people pulled many wet rabbits out of the water. We would not harm any of these animals, but would free them on the island where they would multiply and provide us with food in lean times. We also helped a couple of deer that were exhausted. When we lifted these animals into the boats, they had to have their legs bound with rope. If not, when they gained their strength back they would tear our canoes apart with their sharp hooves and either sink the boat or capsize it. Our people also saved some foxes, lynx, and mink that had their fur singed and had reached the point of exhaustion.

The larger animals like the moose and elk who were strong swimmers had no problems with the river. The wolves and cougars kept ahead of the fire and enjoyed feasting on the smaller animals.

As we paddled upriver, we were amazed at the colours of the fire. Once the fire had burnt itself out, Nokomis would start the renewal with the rains. The woodpeckers would be the first to come back and thrive. They would feast on the bark beetles and other insects that had settled in the newly burnt trees.

Aspen, raspberry, and rose would sprout from underground roots after the fire passed. Moose, elk, and deer would feed on this new growth.

The lodge pole and jack pine have resin-sealed cones that the fire pops open and this scatters their seeds and promotes new growth.

Even though the fire looked like it was destroying all in its path, it missed many green spots and that is where many animals took refuge.

By midmorning we landed on the island and started unloading. We released the animals that we had rescued from the river and they scampered and ran toward the pine, cedar, and maple forests. The women and children started to make shelters and the men went into the forest to bring back saplings and birch needed to build our lodges.

This island was easily defensible with the rapids surrounding it from the north. Anyone who now came up or down the river would have to deal with us.

24

JOURNEY TO THE LAND OF THE OUENDAT

AFTER THE FIRE WE busied ourselves gathering berries, roots, nuts, building new wàginogàns, and hunting for our winter stores. The Ayàbe Tibik-kìzis (Buck Moon, July) soon ended and this became the time when new antlers start to appear on the deer. With the coming of the Wìyagiminan Tibik-kìzis (Fruit Moon, August), we made a decision to travel to the west to visit and trade with our allies the Ouendat. They lived in an area of fertile fields and an abundance of game. We would have to travel to the north up the Kitcisìpi then over to the big lake of the Nippissing people. From there we would take the river that empties into the big bay. There would be many portages, one to three a day. Depending on the weather, we would make it there in twenty to twenty five days.

The Ouendat lived year-round in their communities. They built large lodges called long houses that were seventy-five to a hundred feet long, each house holding forty or fifty people. They also grew what they called the Three Sisters, mandàman (corn), askootasquash (squash), and azàhan (beans).

Our people were mostly nomadic. We hunted, fished, and gathered berries and roots. Breaking the soil and growing our own food was not a priority with us. If we could not pick it or kill it, we traded for what we needed. When we visited our allies the Ouendat, we always traded furs for the Three Sisters and for nasemà. The Ouendat obtained their tobacco from allies called the Petun. The extra buffalo robes that we still had would bring us much needed trade goods. During this time, we would also trade dogs to make our breeds grow stronger. I took the small dog with me because Ishkodewan and he were inseparable. Once the Ouendat see this pair there is the possibility I could receive many offers for both of them, but I would never part with either.

Mitigomij and Wàgosh stayed with the village to look after the safety of the remaining people. Enough warriors will remain with them to defend and hunt for the people. The island was easily defendable and we expected the other bands to be coming to join up with us, in order to gather for the remainder of the summer. The warriors that came with me would have to be strong enough to have only two to a canoe, because each canoe was laden with furs and a dog or two to trade. On the way home, the boats would be full of corn, squash, beans, and tobacco.

I thought carefully about who I wanted to accompany me on this mission. It would take us forty or more suns to travel there and back and there would be another ten or twelve days of feasting. Arrival back to our village would not be until the start of the Kìshkijigewin Tibik-kìzis (Harvest Moon, September).

I knew Kàg and the twins wanted to go. The warrior women and their friend Kànikwe were also good choices. Of course, Mònz would not want to stay behind. Leaving only the Elder Nìjamik to ask and two young warriors to travel with him, Miskwì and Kinòz-I Ininì.

There would be five canoes and eleven warriors. Because of the peace pact with the Nippissing, the journey would be safe from any rivals. Sunrise in two days was our departure. We canvassed the village for furs and dogs to trade. I assigned the twins the responsibility of gathering food for our journey. Unless we came across any game, we would not take time out to hunt.

In the Land of the Haudenosaunee, a conversation was taking place between two warriors.

"Mishi-pijiw Odjìshiziwin (Panther Scar), we have news of a great fire in the Algonquin lands," said Mandàmin Animosh (Corn Dog). "They will have to move from the interior and the riverbanks to safety on the islands; because of this, they will not be as vigilant. Their people will be busy building new lodges and replenishing what they have lost. It might also keep the bands from joining with each other until later in the summer."

"Finally, the time is right to strike these dogs that call themselves warriors and men," said Panther Scar. "They have much to pay for. We will find them, kill their men, burn their lodges, and take their women and children. I want the one with the Black Panther. Everyone thinks he is Michabo the Trickster God and the cat the Fabulous Night Panther. I have met both in battle and still carry the scars to this day. They are neither Gods nor Legends. Call in the warriors. The Haudenosaunee will claim their revenge! We leave in one day. Tell the runners any warrior that cannot make it here is to meet us at the big lake for the crossing up the Kitcisìpi. Tell them this will be a good raid. Tonight we offer tobacco to the Gods and dance and feast."

We started out that morning in a cooling mist. We covered our bodies with grease mixed with goldenseal, to ward off the mosquitoes. The wet mist made our bodies shine in the morning sun. Kàg and Mònz set the pace for us all. There was just a whisper of wind and the river was calm. In these conditions, our small group would make good time.

I was in the front of my boat with my weapons nearby. The warrior in the bow was always responsible for the defence of the canoe. He would always see the danger first and had to be prepared to defend the craft. The small dog and my wolf sat in the middle of the boat with their noses stuck in the air inhaling the smells of the river. With me in the boat was Kànikwe. No words passed between us for the longest time; we just paddled and kept our thoughts in our minds.

"Mahingan, I had a dream last night. I have dreamt the Haudenosaunee would come while we were away."

"Kànikwe, the village is well defended and with Mitigomij and his cat watching over things all will be fine. Furthermore, in the next little while the other bands will be coming for our summer gathering. This will make us too strong for our enemies to want to raid."

Mitigomij was worried. Mahingan was gone now ten suns and only one small band had come for the gathering. Some of the others had sent word that the fire had destroyed their villages and that the other bands were helping them to rebuild and replenish their food stock. Still, this turn of events would make them vulnerable if there was trouble. He had to be cautious, and he needed Wàgosh to spend less time with Kwingwìshì and more on the village security. Needing fresh game, he asked Wàgosh to gather some men and go on a hunt. That way they would also have men out in the woods in case any of our enemies were lurking around.

Panther Scar and his men had been on the warrior trail for seven days. They were now on the Kitcisìpi River. The wind was from the north that day, and it carried with it the smell of the burnt forest. It pleased Panther Scar to know that they were nearing their enemies, the Algonquins. In the next four or five days, they would have scalps, women, and prisoners to torture. After this was over, he would also have the feeble-legged one and his black cat. As he looked back from his canoe, he smiled. There were thirty-eight boats with over a hundred Haudenosaunee warriors.

✻ ✻ ✻

We had been on our journey now for twelve days. During one of our portages we came across a small party of Nippissing warriors that included Ojàwashkwà Animosh, the man that I had defeated in the running race the past summer. Ojàwashkwà Animosh had ten warriors with him, and they were on a hunting trip. When we told him we were travelling to visit our close allies the Ouendat, he asked if he could join us. His people were low on tobacco, and it would be a welcome diversion to trade with these allies from the west. Joining up we continued our travels down the river to the big bay. During this time, the mosquitoes became very bothersome, getting into our eyes and mouths. We pulled ashore and searched in the woods for tree fungus. Within an hour, we had filled four baskets full of the valuable smudge. All of the warriors then inserted it in a short-wedged stick and tied it to our heads. We lit the fungus and the smoke kept the annoying bugs away. Because we had picked the fungus green, there was no danger of fire, and it served as a very effective deterrent to these annoying insects. While gathering the fungus we also obtained some alder bark to treat our underarms, which had scalded from the constant rubbing as we paddled morning to night. When applied to the bruised and scalded area it stung, but it also soon healed the problem.

Upon reaching the mouth of the river, we decided that we would spend a day to rest and hunt fresh meat. The continuing paddling had started to drain our strength and our food stocks were becoming low. Fresh meat would be a welcome respite, and we would use the skin in trade. We sent out two hunting parties, one up each side of the shoreline with the understanding that once the sun was high in the sky each group would turn back toward camp. The remaining warriors would make camp and do any necessary repairs to the canoes.

My group consisted of Ojàwashkwà Animosh and one of his men plus the two warrior women. We had also brought Ishkodewan and the small dog. The mosquitoes were thick as smoke but our smudge sticks kept them at bay. Our path took us along a rocky beach area that seemed to stretch forever. As we were finally coming to the end of this uneven walk, the animals gave a low growl. Ahead we could see a burnt out area from a long ago forest fire, but that was not what caught our attention and caused the wolf and dog to sound the alert.

Panther Scar and his men, after being on the warrior trail for twelve days and the river for five of them, were now nearing the Omàmiwinini lands. The large war party stopped and made camp. Panther Scar then selected two groups of men and sent them out as a probing force to scout ahead looking for any villages. His men had been travelling on dry corn and water during the trek. The corn staved off the hunger pains by swelling the stomach, but fresh meat would strengthen the men and with that in mind, he sent out hunting parties. During the next few days, they feasted, danced, and built up their strength for the battle ahead. When the raid was over, they would retreat down the river and back to their lodges with their captives and scalps.

Mitigomij did not like what was unfolding. The family units were not gathering in force because they were busy trying to replenish what they had lost in the fire. A good majority of the families were not as lucky as they had been with having an available sanctuary on the island. Many of them who had been inland had been able to escape to the middle of small rivers with only what they could carry. Now they were preoccupied with trying to replace what they had lost to the fire with their warriors out hunting and fishing and their women gathering roots and berries. Only three small families had come to the gathering place and even though the island had good defences, Mitigomij was concerned because he only had about thirty-five warriors among the hundred and fifty people under his care. At this time there were two hunting groups of twelve men out, leaving an undermanned force to protect the village.

Wàgosh and his five men had been hunting for two days now. They had a clutch of misise and some mashkodesì (quail) to take back, but what he would have really liked was a deer to make the trip worthwhile. Ever since the fire, the deer had been slow in returning to the fire-ravaged forest. The green shoots of grass had started to sprout through the blackened earth and there were some signs of the animal, but they had not yet been able to sight one. With him were the red and white dogs. They were two skillful hunters, but they had failed to pick up any scent that would have put them on the chase. They were now walking along the riverbank hoping to pick something up there. Just as they had reached a stand of silver birch, the dogs started to growl. Then Wàgosh felt a rush of air passing his head. Turning to see what had caused this sudden breeze, the man behind him gurgled, spat blood on Wàgosh's chest, and dropped dead.

Standing in the knee-high grass I could see a magnificent elk. We were up wind from him, so he had not caught our scent. I put my hand out to quiet the animals. Motioning to Ojàwashkwà Animosh and the others, they stopped in their tracks. We were at least fifty feet out of bowshot and would have to work our way closer to the killing range of our arrows. We crouched down and duck walked to where we could shoot with maximum efficiency. It only took us a few minutes, and we were in range. Together, the five of us rose and let loose our shots. All hit the mark and then I sent Ishkodewan and the small dog in pursuit. An animal this large could run for a long way before it bled out, and we did not want to lose him. The meat would feed our group for the rest of the journey and the hide would bring a lot of tobacco and Three Sisters.

As soon as the arrows struck, the big bull took off with a bellow that made my hair stand on end and my ears ring. The arrows had all hit in the neck and lung area, but this animal was huge, and he would have the strength to give us a good run. The wolf and dog were on the animal before he could make it to the woods and they all crashed through the underbrush with a sound that awoke all the birds and small animals from their midday drowsiness. Our small hunting group broke into a run and the chase was on.

When we hit the forest area, the huge animal had ploughed a path wide enough for us to run two abreast. As we ran through where he had snapped off small trees, trampled berry bushes and thorn trees, we could see clumps of his hair fastened to the broken tree limbs and thorns. His blood was now spattering the trail, and we could see huge spatters of froth on the underbrush. If there were any human activity near us, they would have heard a wolf howling, a dog barking, and a huge elk bellowing in fear and breaking down small trees like a huge wind as he cut a swath through the woods. When we finally caught up to the animals, the dog and wolf had the elk cornered against a rock escarpment. The big bull was down on his two front knees, swinging his huge head so that neither of them could get to him. This preoccupation, however, cost him his life. The two warrior women had circled around him and charged from his back. Before the elk even knew they were there, they had buried their spears in his body behind his front withers, impaling the lungs. With one very huge bellow, he spurted blood out of his mouth toward Ishkodewan and the small dog. The two animals stopped in their tracks and stood stunned, covered in blood from the huge creature. At that moment there was not a sound as men and beasts stood dumbfounded at what had just happened in the blink of an eye. Ojàwashkwà Animosh, the other warrior, and I stood with our spears at the ready. We looked at the two warrior women and the dogs, their bodies red with the animal's blood. Everyone fell silent until Ojàwashkwà Animosh's man reached into his pouch, took out a handful of tobacco, knelt by the huge beast, and gave thanks with a tobacco offering to Kitchi Manitou.

After the offering, we started to butcher the animal and make travois to pull the meat out of the bush. The dog, wolf, and hunters carried the meat and skin out of the bush as we made our way back to camp. We would take as much as we could carry and leave the rest to the forest denizens.

With blood trickling down his neck and chest from the spatter of the man behind him, Wàgosh turned and watched as the man dropped with an arrow impaled in his throat. Turning his attention back to the tree line Wàgosh could see six warriors charging through the forest at them. Wàgosh drew his knife in one hand and his war club in the other and charged at the nearest man. As the enemy neared him, Wàgosh dropped to one knee and drove his knife into the man's thigh. The enemy warrior then caught him with a weak blow on the shoulder with his axe. Infuriated that a wounded adversary had struck him, Wàgosh swung his club as hard as he could on the back of the man's left leg, bringing him down to the ground. Then driving his knife into the side of the man's throat, Wàgosh ripped it forward. Withdrawing the weapon, he noticed his arm completely covered with the other warrior's blood. Taking a quick glance at the dead man, Wàgosh was stunned to see who he was — Haudenosaunee!

The one hunting party that had gone out to the north had been back since the noon sun, but Wàgosh and his men were still out to the south. The northern party had returned with a deer and some geese — enough food for a few days. However, we still needed more. Mitigomij could not spare any more hunters with Wàgosh still absent from the village. He needed as many men as possible for the village's safety. With the family units slow in gathering because of the fire, he feared that there would be trouble and that there would be too few warriors to handle the village's defence.

This fear was based on the premise that the Haudenosaunee would find out about the fire and then take advantage of the turmoil that had beleaguered his people in the days afterwards. Death was always close by if there was an opportunity to strike when the Omàmiwinini were in a weakened state.

After, Ojàwashkwà Animosh, his small party, and I had butchered the wàbidì, we left to go back to the camp on the river. We would eat well that night and dance with the spirit gods. With the added strength of the meat from this great creature, our bodies would enable us to cross the big bay and reach the shores of the Ouendat in a little more than a day. We gave Agwanìwon Ikwe and Kìnà Odenan the heart for their role in the hunt, for making the final kill. These two women never ceased to amaze me with their hunting, paddling, and warrior skills. Then on top of all these skills, they had the compassion of mothers when it came to children, elders, and the welfare of the village. I would take them and their friend Kànikwe over any other ten warriors. To me these three were as loyal, trustworthy, and fierce in battle as my three brothers and brother-in-law.

Wàgosh found himself fighting for his life. The six original attackers had expanded by at least ten more. His small group of five warriors and he were being overwhelmed. Three of his men were dead and the other two were screaming in pain from being hacked to death with spears and knives. After slaying the two Haudenosaunee, Wàgosh found himself forced toward a cliff of about thirty feet with a small creek below that ran into the Kitcisìpi River. Now covered in blood — his own and his enemies — two of the men had lengths of rope with a noose and were intent on capturing him alive. One of the men let his guard down for a moment and Wàgosh was able to slash his arm as he tried to immobilize him with the rope. He then caught him with a glancing blow off his shoulder and onto the side of the man's head. With a whimper, the wounded foe grabbed the side of his head and tried to keep his balance. Wàgosh was now back peddling precariously near the cliff. His mouth was extremely dry, his body clammy. His heart was quickening because he knew he was near either death or worse — captured alive. The remaining three Haudenosaunee were closing in to conclude this incident when two events happened simultaneously. He started to lose his footing and a war club hit him in the ribs with a crunch, knocking the wind out of his whole body with a resounding *whoosh*. As he felt himself falling, the last sounds he heard were the screams of his fellow hunters being hacked to death, along with the snapping of tree limbs. Then his head hit a tree while he was still airborne. Blackness followed.

I woke Ojàwashkwà Animosh and together we brought in the sentries and roused the camp. We had camped on the shoreline of the Big Bay (Georgian Bay) belong to the Ouendat Nation, now we would have to journey the rest of the way by land and carry all our trade goods. The night before, we had pulled our canoes ashore and covered them with brush. Runners had been sent ahead to announce our coming. We knew where the village was, as we had visited two years ago. Unlike the Omàmiwinini, who were constantly on the move, the Ouendat may move a village possibly only every twenty to forty years.

The community that we were heading for was the largest of the eight in the area surrounding the bay. They used a totem of a bear to bond the villages under a clan called Attignawantan. The clan's function was to resolve conflicts among the people, as well as discuss war, defense plans, peace and trade. Overseeing all this was a council that met once a year.

The Ouendat were shrewd traders and travelled by canoe to the Big Water (Hudson Bay) in the north, to the west (now Lake Winnipeg), what is now the Gulf of St. Lawrence and the Chesapeake Bay area. They had many friends and allies but were usually at war with the Haudenosaunee. The land where the Ouendat lived grew wonderful crops of corn, squash, and beans. The Omàmiwinini people were extremely fond of these Three Sisters and considered it a privilege when we could trade for them.

Over half of the Ouendat diet consisted of corn, either dried and shelled or pounded into flour, with which they made unleavened bread. In addition, they made corn soup and like our soups, they added meat, fish and berries to it.

They planted their crops on raised hills. Before planting, they burned the brush in the fields to help fertilize the land. With the crops planted, the women erected lookout towers for them and the older children to keep watch. It was their job to keep the birds away from the freshly sown seeds by creating enough noise to scare them from the new seeding.

In the fall, they harvested the crops and hung them in their longhouses. The corn was stored in pits and covered with grass and earth.

Other than the longhouses and the growing of crops, the Ouendat lived a life very similar to ours. They had specially trained dogs that they used to hunt bears; the small dog's parents came from this village in trade years before from the Ouendat. That is why he was so fearless. Furthermore, like us, they ate their dogs when wild game was scarce.

After we had sent out our runners, we slowly travelled through the forest, burdened down with our trade goods. When the sun was in its mid-afternoon slide to the horizon, we heard a vast uproar of whoops to the front of us. Our runners had brought back twenty or so Ouendat warriors to assist us back to their village. The Ouendat helped lighten our loads, and ceremonially led away with whoops and song.

It was not long until we came out of a stand of glistening white birch into a huge clearing. As far as we could see, was corn taller than a man, with squash and beans growing around the stalks. In the distance our eyes caught sight of a huge palisaded village with wooden walls twenty feet high and smoke rising up in columns from the longhouses dispersing against the crystal blue sky.

We had reached their main village, the centre of the Ouendat Nation.

25

OSSOSSANE

THE VILLAGE OF OSSOSSANE was in the centre of the Ouendat Nation. All the decisions of this Nation became law here.

When you entered the fortification of the Ouendat, the first thing that struck you was the enormity of the enclosure. The palisade itself was made of twenty-foot trees that were three to five inches in diameter. They burnt the poles at the bottom before they put them into the ground so they would not rot when driven into the soil. When erected, they were spaced from six to twelve inches apart and then woven with bark and small branches to close the openings. Along the bulwark they erected watchtowers and defensive galleries that were accessed by ladders. Along the walls of the fortification were large rocks to throw down onto their enemies and reserves of water to douse any fires that their foes would try to start at the bottom of the poles.

After I took my attention away from the defensive structure, the inner village itself aroused my eyes and senses. The smell of meat and their garden produce cooking, interspersed with the aroma of wood burning and the body odours of nearly a thousand people was enough to set me back on my heels. These smells hit me like an impenetrable bramble of brush at a forest's edge. It stopped me in my tracks and I stood along with my warriors stunned by all this and the noise. After spending so much time in the quiet wilderness getting here, the sounds and the smells amazed us and shocked our bodies into a realization that we were such a small amount of life in the whole scheme of things brought forth by Kitchi Manitou.

The Ouendat lived in longhouses that housed lineage all related to the matriarch. At one of these huge houses, we were invited in to eat and tell the story of our journey there. The first thing that I noticed when I walked into the building were the smells that overpowered me when I had entered the village. However, even more overpowering in the smaller confined space were the fragrances of burning wood, tobacco, and the stench of body sweat. My eyes were also starting to sting and water from the lingering smoke of the cooking fires that were constantly going at all hours. The smoke appeared to hover before it escaped from the longhouse, climbing up to the ceiling and out through the smoke hole at the top. Every family had its own fire and there were six fires going in this lodge.

All along the sides were platforms about four feet from the ground. Here they slept on cornhusk mats and furs and stored their food. In the winter, the family members slept beside the fires and along the ceiling hung meat, berries, corn, herbs, and other foods.

For two days we would feast and tell stories before beginning to trade, which would take another two or three days.

Makadewà Wàban came to the large oak tree where Mitigomij was leaning and growled. At the sound of the big cat's warning, Mitigomij's skin raised up into welts. Immediately he let out the warning sound of a pikwàk-ogwewesì to warn his outlying sentries. Only two of the three answered. Mitigomij drew his knife and club and waited for the inevitable.

Even though the island they were on was easily defendable, without the added numbers of the outlying family units, they were spread too thin to protect the stronghold. When Mahingan had left, he was under the assumption that the other families would gather in for the summer meeting and there would be safety in numbers. In addition, after the big forest fire, our hunting parties were foraging father afield, reducing the amount of warriors that were available.

Mitigomij had told his remaining warriors to have their weapons available at all times, even in the village. He had an uneasy feeling and could sense that Nokomis was breathing a warning toward his people.

Mitigomij and the panther hid behind the large oak tree that completely concealed the two of them. He laid his knife and club at the ready and then loaded a stone into his slingshot.

The first Haudenosaunee warrior emerged stealthily from a nearby stand of maples. Mitigomij's aim was quick and sure. The man dropped to the ground with only a short grunt, as the stone had made a hole into the front of his skull the size of a baby's fist. Startled, the intruder behind him stopped for one short pause of breath and this enabled Mitigomij to loosen two arrows immediately. One of the missiles entered the man's left eye socket and the other arrow pinned another warrior's hand to his chest.

Three warriors felled in less time that it takes your heart to beat twice. The remaining five or six opponents caught sight of Mitigomij and charged. Makadewà Wàban met the leading warrior head on with a thundering crash of man and beast. The cat tore out the warrior's throat with one rip of his huge incisors, and then swung one of his massive front paws, breaking another man's leg with a resounding snap of bone, leaving the man screaming and writhing in pain. Mitigomij had been able to get one more arrow off, but he had rushed the aim and it had missed its mark.

Grabbing his knife and war club, he waited for the remaining enemies to reach him. The first man to reach him swung his club and Mitigomij was able to block it with his own weapon. He then drove his knife straight up into the man's left armpit. The victim's blood started to run down his knife and arm before he could withdraw the blade. Then everything went dark....

Ojàwashkwà Animosh and I met with the Ouendat's council. Their Chiefs, Ozàwà Onik (Yellow Arm), Asin

(Stone), and Ogìshkimansì (Kingfisher), talked about trading with us. They also brought up the point of how they valued the Nipissing and us as allies. The biggest concern relayed to us was about the Haudenosaunee, now led by a younger chief, intent on raiding the enemy villages and removing the competition from their hunting grounds north of the big lake. They were pushing the Attiwandaronk from the south. In addition, the Petun also were feeling the wrath of these fierce raiders.

These chiefs wanted to send warriors home with us, on the condition that the Nippissing and the Omàmiwinini would join forces with the Ouendat Nation to strike the Haudenosaunee from the northeast. While the main body of Ouendat, Petun and Attiwandaronk attacked from the northwest. The Ouendat were fearful that if the Haudenosaunee overran the tribes south of them they would be next to feel the wrath of their war clubs. The chiefs were of the opinion that if they struck first at the heart of the Haudenosaunee Nation from two different sides they could put their enemies on the defensive for a while.

I then asked them, "How many warriors would you send home with us?"

"One hundred and fifty, all young and strong," Ozàwà Onik answered, "and I will lead them."

I directed my look to Ojàwashkwà Animosh, and he nodded his head saying, "The Nippissing will pledge one hundred warriors to this war party."

I then replied, "The Omàmiwinini will also contribute one hundred warriors, giving us a very formidable force to deal with our common enemy."

Within the next two days we finished our trading. During this period I turned down many offers for the wolf and small dog. Toward the end of the trading session, an Ouendat offered me six dogs and a boatload of tobacco and corn.

"I am sorry," I replied. "There is not enough trade goods to buy these animals. They are trustworthy companions, experienced hunters, and accomplished guard animals much too valuable to trade. They could never be replaced."

He nodded his head and said, "Mahingan, these dogs are special spirits and will protect you with their lives, leading you out of danger when the hour is at its most crucial point."

The last Ouendat who had tried to trade for the animals was a Shaman and his words carried immense weight with me.

After travelling for twenty-one days, trading and feasting for another six, we were now eager to leave for our homes. Especially with the knowledge that once we reached our lands we would be carrying on to attack our enemy to the south during the fall months. Our trip home would be faster with the extra Ouendat warriors, being able to disperse our goods among the extra canoes, lightening everyone's loads. We would make an impressive force of close to sixty canoes full of men and goods.

The day before we left, we got permission from the Ouendat Chiefs to send out a hunting party to obtain fresh meat for the journey. The hunters would take some young Ouendat boys with them, sending them back to the village with the skins of the slain animals as a gift to the village for letting us hunt from their lands.

As we left, the people of the village came to the front gate and spilled out into the fields to cheer us on our way with songs, whoops, and yells. They knew that some of their warriors would never make it back to their homeland and this brought a wail from their relatives. They then began to sing to make their journey easier. The ones who did come back to the village would be gone for possibly four to six months. During that time their wives would most likely take another man. That was the Ouendat way.

Now my thoughts turned to my village. My heart was heavy with the longing I felt for my wife and child. I prayed that they were safe. I hoped that we could reunite before the Kìshkijigewin Tibik-kìzis. If I had only known what would befall my people in the coming days, my blood would be rushing through my veins as cold as a winter stream! Only death and destruction were in my future. I had no forewarning of the disturbing events that were about to unfold.

As we trotted through the pine, birch, and hardwood forest on the well-worn path to our boats, we came upon a warrior tied to a dead man and a large oak tree. Ozàwà Onik, who was at my side, said that this man had murdered the warrior he was tied to. The Ouendat punishment for this was what we were witnessing. The murderer would slowly starve to death and the victim's family would have their redemption.

Incest, murder, and theft were dealt with by their council and decisions rendered after all parties were heard from. Justice was always swift.

26

DEMISE AND
DEVASTATION

PANTHER SCAR HAD SENT out skirmishers to over-power the outlying sentries stationed around the village. They were to kill the sentries and then send a man back to report that they had accomplished the mission. He would wait until all the runners had returned with word, and then he would send them back with a contingent of warriors to attack. Panther Scar wanted the attack to be from all four sides to prevent any chance of escape by the Omàmiwinini. The attacks would not be coor-dinated, but they would confuse the enemy. Once they rushed to one part of the village to defend it, another group of his men would enter from another direction. The result would be total bedlam for the defenders and an easy victory for Panther Scar.

Three of his runners were back, leaving only one of the groups unaccounted for.

Panther Scar then split his men into four groups and sent them on their murderous quest. Before they left Panther Scar said, "Burn everything. Kill all the warriors, capture the women for wives and slaves, and bring back the young children to raise as our own. We will wipe this village out and leave their bodies for the animals. Leave now and avenge our fallen warriors."

He personally would lead the final group along with Corn Dog to find the missing warriors who had not returned. Motioning for them to follow, they left on a trot to where he had sent the missing skirmishers. In twenty minutes, they came upon a small clearing. There lay eight of his best warriors dead and dying. Four of them looked like they had been mauled by a wild animal as they lay on the ground in their own blood, with their throats ripped out. Their eyes were open and all their faces had a complete look of shock and horror.

Two men were still alive. One warrior, He Who Runs, had his hand pinned to his chest with an arrow that was protruding from his back. It would take a tremendous amount of strength and a bow of immense proportions to do this kind of damage to a man. He was bleeding to death from the wound. Sheer terror showed in his face. No words emitted from his lips. His face was ashen and he was at death's entrance.

"Panther Scar, help me," a feeble voice called out.

Panther Scar and his men turned to see a young warrior named Grouse Feather, his leg a bloody mess, lying in a pool of blood.

"Who did this to you? Were you and the others ambushed by an overpowering force?"

"No, Panther Scar. Only one man with a withered leg and a black demon of a panther!"

"Grouse Feather, you cannot tell me one man killed all of these Haudenosaunee warriors, a cripple at that?" said Corn Dog.

"Oh, mighty chief, this man and his cat are either demons or gods. They fight like both and kill without mercy!"

Panther Scar knew who the man was that his young warrior was talking. The big cat had left him with the scars that he now wore for life. This lone warrior spared his life that day many years ago at the small stream, but he still could not believe this man and his cat were invincible. Panther Scar still carried the hatred for this warrior they called Mitigomij. To have your life spared by an enemy was a curse that you had to carry with you the rest of your life. He owed him his life, but also carried the scorn that his people cast on him for years until he could prove that he was not a coward, but a strong warrior and a decisive leader.

"Grouse Feather, how could eight warriors not kill this man?"

"He slew two of the warriors and fatally wounded He Who Runs before we even knew what was happening. Then the big cat went to work. Ripping out Standing Man's throat and breaking my leg. The other three reached the lame one, and he killed the first to reach him with a knife to his armpit. I then watched as Black Owl and Pointed Nose clubbed him into unconsciousness, but then the big cat killed them both in an instant. After that, I thought I was hallucinating. The panther grabbed the back of the lame one's shirt and lifted him up like a bitch dog grabs a pup and carried him off into the woods!"

"Was he dead?" asked Panther Scar.

"That I don't know. He took some powerful blows to his body and head from our two warriors before the black demon cat killed them. What are these two? They fight like nothing I have ever seen before. Who trains a wild animal like this to fight along side of them? They have to be shape changers! They are invincible."

"I don't know, Grouse Feather, but someday if he is still alive I'll reap my revenge from him."

"I'll leave a man with you to splint your leg and to stem the blood flow from the wound. When the battle is over, I will send someone back for the two of you, but you will have to keep up with us when we leave or die in this country. You know a warrior's fate when wounded."

Panther Scar then led his warriors to the carnage that was to befall Mahingan's village of over a hundred souls.

The three chiefs Mahingan, Ojàwashkwà Animosh, and Ozàwà Onik and their flotilla had reached the bay at dusk where they had left the canoes previously and now were camped for the evening.

Mahingan was enjoying a feast of deer. He reached into the birch bark container full of squash, corn, beans, and meat, scooping out more of the watery soup with the wooden bowl he always carried. Then with his hand he shovelled the lukewarm broth into his mouth. As he ate and talked, juice ran out the corner of his mouth and he wiped it away with the back of his hand. The smoke of the fire mixed with the smell of the men's body odours and their occasional flatulence caused his nostrils to flare with the pungency of it all.

"We were over twenty days coming here. I would like to cut that down to fewer than twenty if we can. With the extra men and food we have now, we will not have to stop and hunt. Ojàwashkwà Animosh will be sending a group of his men off to bring Nipissing warriors into our war party. When we get near our village, I will send men to ask the Innu, Maliseet, and Abenaki to join us at the big rapids. This will give us a force of over six hundred warriors for the battle."

"Mahingan," said Ozàwà Onik, "with the strength of this force we will be able to set the Haudenosaunee back for years."

That morning we rose at dawn, ate quickly, and left as the sun was starting to rise. There was a slight briskness to the morning and Mahingan could smell the pines and cedar through the early morning mist. He loved this time of day before the sun heated up the earth. He could taste the freshness of the clean air. When they were in their boats, the water was so clear and blue that they could see the bottom of the bay. Fish swam by and once they saw a huge nàme (sturgeon) almost the size of the boat. He would have liked to stop and try to spear this monster, but they were setting a brisk pace and they did not need any food at this time.

In his canoe were the twins. They carried the weight of warriors now, lean and well muscled. Both had shaved half of their heads and had tattoos on their faces. Their bodies glistened with bear grease mixed with goldenseal to ward off the bugs.

With this band of warriors well fed and strong, we would be home before the next moon.

Wàgosh woke in a pouring rain. His head throbbed. He was having trouble breathing because of a dislocated rib. Taking a piece of wood, he gritted it between his teeth to help dull the pain, and then probing with his fingers, he found the misaligned bone. It did not feel broken, but it was causing extreme pain and shortness of breath. Clenching his fist, he hit the rib as hard as he could. Immediately, he could feel a rush of cool air into his lungs as the rib snapped back into place. The sharp end of a war axe had struck him, opening a wound the size of his fist. The blood was still seeping from this gash. His body was scratched and torn from the fall and covered with the blood that was trickling out of cuts and abrasions. The redness of the blood mixed with the rain covered his whole body in a deathly pale crimson colour. Wàgosh opened his medicine bag and, taking out a bone needle and deer sinew, prepared to work on his wounds. First he needed something to stem the bleeding. He had fallen into a ravine that had a stream flowing through it and a small meadow. He was sore and dizzy. Luckily none of his appendages were broken, but when he stood his surroundings started to spin. He dropped to his knees in pain and bewilderment. Taking a deep breath he knew that unless he could treat his injuries he would die beside this stream and his body would be food for the animals. Opening his eyes through the pain, he caught a glimpse of a patch of yellow flowers. Stumbling to the area, he dug up the plant. He popped the roots into his mouth and ate for subsistence. He washed his wounds with water from the stream and then, using the juice from the stems of the shìwanìbìsh (dandelion), he treated his lesions; this would stop the bleeding and help heal the gashes. Then he took the needle and, threading the sinew into it, proceeded to close the larger cuts. He started on his forehead, then his arms, working his way down to his legs. When he finished, he had counted over forty times he had stitched his skin. After he was done, he reached into his mouth and removed two of his teeth that were just hanging from their sockets. He was now too sore to move and the rain was cleansing the blood from his body and cooling the soreness of his damage. Reaching into his warrior's bag, he removed some jimsonweed and made poultices with what moss he could collect. His head felt like someone was pounding on it with a large rock. He crawled to a large pine tree and pulled himself under it, seeking shelter from the rain. The pine needles provided some comfort from the ground, and then he passed out from the pain.

By the time Panther Scar had reached the Algonquin village, the slaughter had started. Less than thirty warriors were there to defend the inhabitants. What were left of them was now protecting a group of women and children huddled in the centre of the encampment. They were being hacked to death by a warrior called Stone Dog and his followers. Screaming women were trying to fend off his warriors with their skinning knives, pieces of wood, and canoe paddles.

As Panther Scar waded into the battle, a young warrior attacked him with a bloody spear. He side-stepped the lunging man and swung with all his might at the side of the boy's head. It ended up being only a glancing blow, but it staggered his foe and sent him to one knee. Panther Scar then grabbed his war club with both hands and brought it down on the man's shoulder. He could hear the shoulder blade break with a resounding crack. Then he grabbed the man's hair and, turning his face to him, spat in it. Then with one fluid motion, he drew his knife and sliced the young warrior from ear to ear. With blood gushing onto his chest, he let the boy drop. As he turned back to the battle, he caught sight of three of his men hacking off the fingers of an overweight Algonquin elder. The man never said a word; he just leered at his men as they went about their horrific job. When they were finished with his fingers, they cut off his ears. Then they left him to bleed to death.

The ground was red with blood. The screams of the women and children as they courageously fought to avoid capture filled the air. Very few Algonquin warriors remained alive. Those that lived were being tied to poles and put into fires.

Corn Dog came to him with two bloody scalps from his victims. "This has been a great victory, my war chief! We have many women and children to take back to our villages for slaves. The fires will soon be put to the remaining men."

Above Corn Dog's voice, he could still hear the women sobbing and crying out for their men. The Algonquins being tortured were screaming out, calling the men "cowards" and "dogs."

"Corn Dog, something is wrong here. There must be more warriors! With this many women and children there has to be another twenty or more men. Have our warriors ready to go by the first light. Then we will travel back to the south."

"Panther Scar, give me thirty warriors. I will raid to the north in another two or three days."

"I don't know, friend. I feel trouble coming, and I want to be far away from here. The lame one and his panther are still alive, and the hunting parties that are out will come back to this village. Once they come upon what we have done to their community, they will follow us and snipe at our men creating havoc on the way back to our homes."

"Great chief, give me these warriors, and I can ravage this country. Look how easily we defeated this weak village. Their men fight like women!"

"Corn Dog, you can leave in the morning. Hand pick your men, but do not venture out from here more than three days. I will be looking for you before we reach the big rapids. The prisoners that you take will have to travel swiftly, as I cannot jeopardize my warriors by waiting for you."

27

THE RECKONING

WÀBANANANG KNEW SOMETHING WAS wrong when the two dogs that were with Wàgosh came back to the village alone. There were spots of fresh blood on the white dog and the red dog was cowering when they entered the camp. These dogs would never leave the hunters unless something traumatic had taken place; neither of these animals ever backed down from a fight. Immediately, she thought of her son, Anokì. If there was danger coming, she had to put him in a safe place. Gathering up her son, some smoked venison, and a fur robe, she rushed into the woods, calling the two dogs to follow her. Wàbananang had to find a safe place away from the village for her son, enabling her to go back and help her people defend their homes if there was an approaching menace. Before long, she reached the place that she had been seeking, a thick stand of cedars surrounding a jumble of rocks and boulders. Here was a small cave formed by a rockslide from many years ago. There was just enough space in the enclosure for her son and the two dogs. Since the day Anokì was born, the two dogs took it upon themselves to be his protectors. They would lie beside him all the time when they were not off on a hunt. Once Anokì started crawling, they steered him away from the fire pits and any other perceived dangers. Wàbananang laid cedar boughs in the cave and then put the fur robe on top. Setting her son on the nest she had made, she gave him the piece of meat to chew on to keep him occupied and quiet. She then fed the dogs and directed them to lie beside Anokì, giving them the signal to stay and keep quiet. After covering up the entrance, she retraced her steps using a cedar branch to erase any sign that they had been there. Then quietly stealing away, she silently prayed to Kitchi Manitou to keep her son safe.

Nearing the village, she could hear the unmistakable noises of a battle. Then off to her left, about a hundred yards or so, she could hear the sounds of warriors scurrying through a stand of birch and pine.

Lying on her stomach, she watched them rise up from their crouching positions, and then with a blood-curdling scream that sent chills through her body, they attacked the village. Wàbananang froze in fear, not knowing whether to return to her son or to come to the aid of the village. Covered in sweat, her heart was beating so rapidly that it was causing her to gasp for air. Never had she been so afraid and horrified in her life. Her immediate thoughts turned to her husband Mahingan.

She knew that if he were here there'd be nothing to fear. The man that was her lifelong love would protect her and Anokì.

Lying there frozen in time, a hand grabbed her by the hair and forced her to her feet. The suddenness of the action caused her neck to feel like he had wrenched it from her shoulders. She could smell the man's pungent breath and body odour as he pulled her face to an inch of his. The smell of the man, along with his painted and tattooed face, brought her to her senses and released a hidden rage, causing her body to explode with a sudden force she had never before experienced. In one motion, she swept her skinning knife from its leather scabbard and drove it into the warrior's hip. Letting out a piercing scream, he drove his fist into Wàbananang's face. She could hear and feel her nose break with the impact of his fist. Gasping for breath and spewing blood from her mangled nose, Wàbananang drove her knife into the man's left bicep, ripping it toward her. Wàbananang's face and body were drenched with blood from herself and her assailant. She was now starting to feel weak from the blow to her face and the original wrenching of her neck. Then her foe released his grip on her hair, grabbed his war club from his waist belt, and swung with a powerful backhanded motion, striking her on the side of her head. Wàbananang's ear was ringing and her jaw felt like it was going to come out the other side of her face. Dropping to one knee, she drove the knife into his groin, all the way up to the bone handle, and then they both fell into a bloody mangled heap.

❈ ❈ ❈

The Ouendat and Omàmiwinini were now only two days from Mahingan's home. Ojàwashkwà Animosh had left the group when they had reached Lake Nippissing.

On his departure Ojàwashkwà Animosh said, "Mahingan and Ozàwà Onik, I will arrive in five or six suns after you get to the village. With me will be a hundred of our best warriors, and we will be prepared to travel immediately after arriving."

That day when we put ashore there were still a couple of hours of daylight left. Kànikwe approached where Kàg and I were building a fire and told us that he and the two warrior women were going out to see if they could find some fresh game. With what Mònz and the twins, who were out in a canoe fishing, could catch, it would enable us to throw a feast for the Ouendat before we entered the village in the next day or so.

Kàg and I carried on with our job after Kànikwe and the women left. The twins and Mònz came to shore a while later with three baskets of fish and a beaver. Everyone pitched in to gut and filet the fish, and skin the beaver for the cooking fires. The dogs and Ishkodewan received the heads to eat and the innards we put in a separate clay pot with roots and berries to make a soup. We impaled the beaver on a spit to roast. We then cut small branches and laid them in a pile. The branches we would then use to skewer the filleted fish and roast them over the fires.

Just as dusk was approaching, Agwanìwon Ikwe called out from the trees, "We are coming in."

Kìnà Odenan and Kànikwe were carrying a deer on a pole between them, and I could see two extra men following them.

"We welcome the three of you back to camp as successful hunters. I see though that you have brought back more than just an anìdjànìl (doe)."

Once the group left the shadows of the forest and entered into the firelight, I could make out the face of Ajowà-Okiwan of the Nibachis Omàmiwinini tribe.

He approached my brother and me with tears in his eyes. "Mahingan, I have terrible news."

The big cat laid beside Mitigomij, licking the warrior's bloodied forehead.

Mitigomij's head and shoulder were throbbing with intense pain, and he could taste blood with a mixture of vomit in his mouth. He had no idea how much time had elapsed since his encounter with the Haudenosaunee warriors. His heart was beating mightily with a burning rage for this foe, and he felt a deep sadness for he could only guess what had happened to his village. Tears stung his eyes. Mitigomij looked around at his surroundings and realized he was in the small cave that he had raised the big cat in. The panther had returned the favour to him by saving his life and bringing him to the only sanctuary that the cat had ever known. The man had no recollection of what had transpired after he had passed out, but only knew that his constant companion had looked after him, as he himself had looked after the cat when it was young and vulnerable.

Mitigomij thought that maybe only part of a day had transpired since his conflict with the Haudenosaunee. His wounds were still seeping, even though the panther had been licking them. Making his way to the cave entrance, he peered out into the night and felt a gush of cool air hit his face, bringing along with it the wonderful smells of the forest that awakened his senses. It also made him realize that he had failed his people in the defense of the village. The early summer fire had dispensed the Omàmiwinini people and prevented them from gathering for the rest of the warm weather and early fall months. This also brought the realization that even though the island was easily defensible, there were not enough warriors to protect against any type of concerted enemy action. The Haudenosaunee had picked their time well, and if they had a couple hundred warriors, they could devastate the scattered Omàmiwinini Nation. Knowing that whatever had transpired was now beyond his control, Mitigomij decided to attend to his wounds and rest. In the morning he and Makadewà Wàban would return to the carnage and wait for his brothers to return from the land of the Ouendat. Then the real bloodletting would begin, in earnest. Mahingan would gather what warriors he could and chase these intruders into the abyss of war.

After coming into the camp we shared with the Ouendat, Ajowà Okiwan related to them what had transpired for the past month.

Ajowà Okiwan and his people arrived about a half moon after we had left for the Ouendat Nation. With him, he had brought his family unit plus all the women, children, and elders of Pangì Shìshìb's family unit of the Matàwackariniwak. Pangì Shìshìb and his warriors were travelling toward the west where the fire had burned, to see if there were any Omàmiwinini people, and if they needed help to come to the summer gathering.

Ajowà Okiwan then told the gathered warriors, "Once we arrived in the village, the populace totalled about one hundred and seventy-five people, which included only about thirty-five warriors. After our arrival, Wàgosh and I decided that we must send out a couple of hunting parties. Each of us took five men, which left the village lightly defended, but the people needed food. Wàgosh took his men to the southern part of the island, and I headed to the main shore and then north with my hunting party.

"We had been out four days and were very successful: two deer, several rabbits, and over forty waterfowl. Laden down with all the game that we had obtained, we were slow in returning to the river and our canoes. When we reached the Kitcisìpi where we had hidden our boats, we noticed a lot of smoke that was too widely dispersed to be cooking fires. It was early morning and the mist was just starting to burn off from the heat of the sun. Then we saw them. Haudenosaunee warriors! There were close to one hundred of them in their canoes leaving the village. Each of the boats had captive women and children in them, except for ten canoes that held only warriors. That group paddled up toward the rapids and then went ashore at the portage and continued north.

"Mahingan, we were greatly outnumbered, and it was all that I could do to keep my men from firing on these boats as they continued downstream from us. A few of them could see wives, children, and sisters in the enemy canoes. Lying in the underbrush as they went by one man in a lead canoe stood out from the rest. The left side of his face and shoulder had deep scars, as if a bear had attacked him and torn his flesh away.

"The main group, I knew would be heading to the south. However, I had suspicions about the other smaller breakaway group. I sent four of my men to trail them along the shoreline with instructions to stay out of sight. Kòkòkòhò (Owl) and I then jumped in a canoe and went to the village. There were no survivors. All the men were dead, killed in battle, or staked in the fires. The Haudenosaunee had done their job well. We then came for you and to strike my axe on the war post!"

I could feel the blood leave my face. My knees weakened and my mouth dried up.

Then I started to sing the Omàmiwinini death song for all who had died. After that I sang for my son, wife, and brothers. When I was done, I reached deep into my soul and cried out an ancient war song my father had taught me. By the time I had finished, the Ouendat and my Omàmiwinini warriors were gathering around me.

I then turned and said at the top of my voice, "Ozàwà Onik, are you and your Ouendat warriors united with us to avenge our families' deaths at the hands of the Haudenosaunee?"

My answer came in one large crescendo of a throaty Ouendat whoop that echoed through the forest and across the river. If there were a man or beast within miles, this eerie sound crashing and tumbling through the air would send shudders through their bodies, causing their hair and skin to rise up in fright. Then they would hope that whoever originated this unworldly cry was not coming for them!

"Light the fire! Tonight we raise the war post and strike it with our weapons," I said. "In the morning we will be the hunters. Paint your faces and bodies and ask Kitchi Manitou for his protection or nothing less than a warrior's death."

Into the night the warriors sang, danced, painted their bodies, and told tales of past battles fought.

At first light me and Ozàwà Onik split the camp into two groups. They sent the twins along with one hundred Ouendat to take the supplies down the waterway to the village. Once there they were to bury all the dead and to wait for their return.

I also told the twins, "When Pangì Shìshìb and his people arrive, have him send some of his warriors south to the land of the Innu and Malecite, asking them to meet us at the big rapids where the two large rivers meet with all the warrior's they can spare. There we will bring all our forces together to strike the Haudenosaunee in their villages to the south before winter settles in."

Ozàwà Onik and I then led the remaining fifty Ouendat warriors and ten Omàmiwinini warriors north to seek and hunt down the thirty Haudenosaunee who had broken off from the main party.

I had sent Kànikwe and the two warrior women ahead of the main group to act as scouts. They then set out of camp on a trot, following a well-worn game and hunting trail that would enable them to cover twenty-five to thirty miles a day. Every two hours they stopped for a quick bite of food and water to sustain their strength and stamina. It had been two days since Ajowà Okiwan had said that the Haudenosaunee had attacked the village, and now they were on a collision course with Corn Dog and his warriors.

28

THE PURSUIT

WE HAD RUN THROUGH the forest for the full day and had neared the Kitcisìpi River. Reaching the river, we encountered our scouts, Kànikwe, and the women, with one of Ajowà Okiwan's men, Okanisì (Grosbeak).

"Okanisì, what news do you bring?" asked Ajowà Okiwan.

"We trailed the Haudenosaunee up the river as you asked us for two days. The enemy had come upon a small fishing party of Nippissing; we were in no position to warn them because our foes had reached the camp long before we knew it was there. Slowed down by the terrain, we came upon the skirmish not long after the event and just in time to see the Haudenosaunee celebrating. It had been a slaughter. The Nippissing only had six warriors that we could make out from our vantage point and the rest were women and children.

It looked like they had been there to fish and hunt for a couple of days because there were not any permanent shelters, just lean-tos and drying racks for the fish they were catching. From our hiding spot, we watched as they loaded their captives and plunder into the canoes. All the boats were in the water except for two, when the men who were shoving off got struck down by a hail of arrows, followed by a group of Nippissing rushing out from the forest cover. The remaining warriors could push off, but not before the Nippissing had filled the two boats with arrows, killing or wounding the occupants. The other canoes escaped to the river out of range of the Nippissing bows.

"When we came out of our hiding spot and approached the Nippissing, we realized it was Ojàwashkwà Animosh. We then told him what had happened to our people south of here on the island.

"Ojàwashkwà Animosh had seventy warriors with him, and a young girl had told them of what had happened at this small camp. She had escaped during the initial attack and had run back toward the main village a few miles away. She was his niece and all the people in the camp were his relatives who had come here to fish for several days.

"Ojàwashkwà Animosh and his men along with our three warriors were following the Haudenosaunee down the river and keeping out of sight. There will be very little they can do because they had no boats enabling them to chase the enemy. The Haudenosaunee will just camp on the islands and not come to shore knowing full well they can't be attacked as they travel downstream and take their portages on the east side of the river."

"Okanisì," I said, "We need you to go back to Ojàwash-kwà Animosh and ask him and his men to try and keep up with the enemy. When they get close enough to them, they are to come out into the open, showing themselves to the enemy, forcing our foe to speed up. When this happens, he can let them think they are out distancing them. We need the Haudenosaunee to think that their only danger is behind them and not ahead. Once they think they have put enough of a gap between the two bodies of warriors their leader will relax. There will be no reason for them to panic, because they will think that they have outdistanced Ojàwashkwà Animosh and his men, and they know that they destroyed the village. With all the risk gone, they should then take the easier portage on the island where we will be waiting with over two hundred Ouendat and Omàmiwinini warriors and another seventy Nippissing warriors closing in behind.

"Go now, Okanisì, and tell Ojàwashkwà Animosh this plan. We will turn back to our village and lay the trap. This enemy force has one day left to live, and then we will turn our attention to the Scarred One."

It was always the strategy of any attacking force to strike from ambush. A successful surprise assault always limited casualties and increased the enemies' loss of life. Very rarely did two opposing forces meet in open battle. The risk of an immense loss of life heightened in head-to-head battle. Ambushes were much more successful.

Mahingan, Ozàwà Onik, and Ajowà Okiwan called their men together and relayed the plan. They now had to hurry to the village and gather the rest of the Ouendat and the twins. The island had to look uninhabited. The rapids there were too dangerous to navigate, and they did not want them to be spooked, land on the eastern shore and disappear into the wilderness.

Me and my group reached the island early the next morning. The twins, Makwa and Wàbek, relayed to us that all the men, old women, and elders were murdered. The Haudenosaunee had put most of the heads on stakes and then threw several of the bodies into the fires. All the remains that they found, they buried. There had been no sign of Mitigomij, Wàgosh, Wàbananang, or Anokì.

Tears welled up in my eyes, my heart ready to burst. "Ishkodewan, small dog, come." I had a hunch that my wife and child had hidden and I needed these two animals to help in the search.

"Ajowà Okiwan and Ozàwà Onik, prepare the warriors and hide all the canoes. I will be back. The enemy will have to portage up from the village at the far northern end of the island."

The wolf, dog, twins, and I then took off at a trot to search for my family. A few spots quickly came to my mind that my wife might use as a hiding spot.

"Ishkodewan, find Anokì!"

At that command, the wolf shot into the lead, followed closely by the small dog. In a matter of minutes we reached a grove of cedars and a rockslide where the wolf started to howl and move toward the rocks. Subsequently we heard the sound of barking from within the rockslide. Then the red dog emerged from a small opening and barked a welcome to his friends. Following the animal's lead, the twins and I reached the opening. Upon peeking in, we caught sight of my son nestled up to the white dog sound asleep. As I reached in and took hold of my son, a great sense of relief overtook my body. I then reached into his pouch and took out some dried meat for the boy, then gave him some water from my clay flask. Anoki never said a word, he just looked up and hugged me. But where was my precious wife Wàbananang? Why would she leave her son here alone? My body then began to shake and tears streamed down my face. Was she dead, captured, or burnt in the fires? My life would never be the same without her. She was my rock. Embracing my son, I dropped to my knees and sobbed uncontrollably. My nephews stood by, dumbfounded. They had never seen me so vulnerable like this. Silently they walked up to me and embraced the man they looked up to as a leader and protector. Now was the time for them to show me that I was not alone and that they cared.

I put my son down. I told him that I would have to leave him here with the wolf and dogs and that I would come back for him later. The boy nodded and crawled back into the small opening followed by the white dog. Then Ishkodewan and the other two dogs lay down outside the entrance.

Turning to the twins I said, "Come. We have to go back to the river. There is something we have to finish."

Returning toward the village, we searched for any sign of my wife. It wasn't until they were almost back to the community that we came upon a pool of blood. Upon closer inspection of the area, I found Wàbananang's bloodied skinning knife. Nevertheless, this did not supply me with the answer I was seeking: was she alive or dead? The amount of blood in the vicinity clearly pointed out that a fatality had taken place here. Seeing the drag marks of a body caused my skin to go clammy and a chill run through my bones. I summarized my wife had died there defending her child's hiding place and they had dragged her corpse to the fires. Tears welled in my eyes until my sight blurred.

Bringing myself back to my senses, I called out to the twins.

"Let's continue."

Travelling along the path to the portage, we could see no sign of anyone, until out of thin air Ozàwà Onik appeared and startled us.

"My friend, the warriors are well hidden. Even the twins and I could not find them!"

Laughing, Ozàwà Onik said, "Wasn't that the plan?"

"Did you find your wife and son?"

"Not my wife, but thanks be to Kitchi Manitou I found my son. Anokì, by the bravery of his mother, spared him certain capture. He is well and protected now by a very loyal pack of dogs and their equally devoted wolf companion. He will be well cared for until my return."

"Ajowà Okiwan and I have all the warriors positioned. A runner arrived from Ojàwashkwà Animosh saying that the Haudenosaunee would arrive late in the afternoon. Ojàwashkwà Animosh said he would be leaving enough men to follow at the rear of the enemy, making them believe that there was a full force behind. He added that his main force would be arriving ahead of the enemy and would conceal themselves above the rapids to prevent any escape to the land on the west bank."

The afternoon dragged on with the warriors shielded from the heat of the day in their hiding places, having to contend with a steady onslaught of stinging insects. We could not risk building smudge fires, so we made do with their goldenseal and bear grease mixtures. Toward the late afternoon Ojàwashkwà Animosh swam the river and told us that his men were in place, along with the news that the Haudenosaunee were very close.

Communicating down the line in whispers, the men had to let the first three canoes land without incident; we needed the enemy to suspect nothing out of the ordinary.

Just as the sun was approaching the tops of the tall pines, we heard the sound of canoes and men coming down the river. The only nervousness from the group was from the rear canoes as we kept looking back for Ojàwashkwà Animosh's men.

In the distance we could hear the sounds of jays and crows warning of the approaching men. This scared a flock of geese from the water; as they were lifting off a few of the warriors brought down three of the birds. Two of the canoes broke off to pick up the fowl and simultaneously the first boat glided into the portage landing.

Corn Dog was hurrying his men toward the portage. The attack on the Nippissing had reaped them a few women and children but cost him one warrior during the initial conflict and six more during the surprise attack as they were departing onto the river. The speed of their canoes and the current of the river enabled them to stay ahead of their pursuers, but this portage was critical. They would have to complete it with the utmost urgency and paddle through the night with torches to try to gain a distance advantage. He figured they were outnumbered two or three to one, but they had the advantage of the river.

Corn Dog watched as the first three of his eight boats landed. Just as he was approaching shore, he caught the glimpse of a small movement in the trees.

"Ambush!" he screamed at the top of his voice.

As soon as the words left his mouth he heard a crack like a frozen tree in the winter, he watched as the man in front of him had his cheek explode in a gush of blood.

"Slingshot," he muttered to himself.

When he turned to look toward the initial noise, he watched as the other warrior's left eye burst from its socket; both men lurched to one side in death spasms causing the canoe to tip over and spill him into the water. As he hit the churning river, he could hear the sound of a panther's scream, sending chills through his body.

From his hiding place, I could see the fear on the Haudenosaunee warriors' faces as they looked toward the sound of the cat's screams. I had a smile on my face knowing Mitigomij was alive. My brother had killed two men in lightning succession.

The signal was given and two hundred warriors screamed from the woods, letting loose their arrows in a volley of death. It caught the enemy by surprise, but the initial alarm had enabled the two boats that were gathering the geese to escape toward the east shore and out of the reach of Ojàwashkwà Animosh and his men's arrows. During their flight, I noticed that they assisted one of their own from the river. I motioned to Ozàwà Onik and pointed out to the river at the fleeing canoes. Immediately he and about twelve of his warriors launched four canoes to try to capture them.

Ojàwashkwà Animosh and some of his men were swimming out to the canoes to aid in the rescue of their people who were captives. Miraculously, they had all survived; once the onslaught had started the captives had lain down in their boats to protect themselves from the arrows. Most of them were in the water, as the boats they were in had tipped over during the battle. The river was running red with blood from the dead. On the shore, the Ouendat had captured three unfortunate warriors who were now singing their death songs.

The Ouendat took the three men into the forest to get information from them to help find the rest of the war party that had destroyed the village.

Kàg, Mònz, and I approached Mitigomij and embraced him.

"Have you seen Wàgosh?" he asked.

Kàg answered, "No, but his body hasn't been discovered either."

As Corn Dog surfaced from the water in a hail of arrows and gasping for air, he turned his attention toward reaching the eastern bank of the river. It would be his only chance of escape. Taking a deep breath of air, he dove under the water to stay hidden from the archers on shore. Swimming until he felt his lungs would burst, he resurfaced beyond the range of their bows and started to swim on the surface. He was still a few hundred yards from shore when the sound of men straining and paddles striking the water echoed behind him. Without breaking his swimming rhythm, he turned his head and saw two canoes of his men pulling along side him. He grabbed the back of one of the boats and held on as his men exerted themselves to escape to the shore. Kicking with his feet to try and not be an encumbrance to the paddlers, he took a quick glance behind. What he saw made an acid reflux reaction in his throat. Four canoes! And they were coming fast! His legs started to weaken in fear; death was near unless his men and he could reach the shore.

Ozàwà Onik and his warriors were closing in fast on the two canoes ahead. He caught a glimpse of one man in the water hanging on to the last boat and kicking furiously. If their enemy reached the shore ahead of them, they would have the advantage of high ground and concealment. Sweat glistened on his body as his muscles burnt to the strain of the chase. Water and perspiration covered his arms and hands, making it difficult at times to hold on to the paddle. His force numbered twelve and he counted five in the boats and one in the water. The one boat with the man in the river had three paddlers and was at least a hundred feet ahead of the other. He knew that his men would overtake the trailing vessel.

The lead Haudenosaunee boat had reached the shore as Ozàwà Onik and his men pulled two abreast to the other boat. The pair in the enemy boat stood and swung their war clubs at their foes and in the short battle that ensued fell under a hail of blows from their opponents' axes. Both slid into the water and their canoe drifted away with the current toward the distant rapids. The warriors who had made the shore turned and shot one volley of arrows. Two of the projectiles fell harmlessly into the river and the other embedded itself in the bow of Ozàwà Onik's boat with a thud. Ozàwà Onik looked toward shore and the men where disappearing into the pine and white birch forest.

"Leave them," he said. "They are more bother than they are worth. They are far from home, and we may still have our way with them before the next two moons are done!"

Kàg and Mònz held out hope that their wives Kinebigokesì and Mànabìsì had survived the attack and were captives. They knew the enemy would have not taken Wàgosh's wife, Kwìngwìshì, because of her pregnancy. They would slay her in the village; a pregnant woman slows down a retreating force.

That night we could hear the screams of the three enemy warriors as the Ouendat tried to obtain information from them. The Ouendat promised them that when they got the information they needed, they would die an honourable warrior's death. No more torture.

We had decided that our band of warriors would leave by the early morning if we had any hope of catching this large retreating force. There was almost a four-day gap between our foe and us, but we would be travelling light and fast. We sent out an advance guard of thirty men to hunt out the Haudenosaunee. It was a five-day warrior's journey to the rapids, but the enemy would probably take seven and possibly wait one or two days for their trailing force. We had to do this journey in four days to try to catch them before they entered their territory. Our hopes were also with our runners, hoping that they could find the Malecite and Innu.

After the battle had ended, Kànikwe and the warrior women had gone out looking for Wàgosh.

During this time, I searched out Nìjamik, the elder who had travelled to the Ouendat land with us.

"Nìjamik, I am going to give you my son Anokì and the two dogs that were with him. I need you to care for him until my return, whenever that may be."

"I will be honoured to look after your son Mahingan," he replied.

Then I called Mikkwì (Blood), Kinòz-i Ininì, and the two twins to a meeting.

"The four of you will be responsible for Mitigomij at all the portages. You will have to carry him in a litter. He will not like it, but he will understand the reasoning behind it. Mitigomij wants to come on this war party, so we will respect his wishes and the four of you will now be able to pay him back for all the training he has given you over the years. The twins will be in the same canoe as their uncle and the big cat. You other two will ride with the wolf and me."

In unison they all said that they would accept the responsibility that I handed them.

As the camp was starting to stir in the early morning and the cooking fires brought to flame, the men heard an honour song from far south of the camp. Kànikwe and the warrior women were entering the camp with a travois. On it was the body of Wàgosh!

"Mahingan, we found him in a ravine under a pine tree. He had tried to nurse his wounds, but he bled to death. It was a warrior's death, and we are sorry to bring you his cold body," said Kànikwe.

"A brother, a sister-in-law, and a wife had been killed in this raid. The Scarred One will pay dearly for this," I whispered to no one and everyone.

We buried our brother on the island beside his wife. After the burial, the combined force of over two hundred and fifty Ouendat, Nippissing, and Omàmiwinini prepared to leave. We left the word with Nìjamik to inform Pangì Shìshìb and Minowez-I to follow behind the war party with what warriors they could spare.

Once we were on the river, I looked back to the island. Little did I know that it would be over three hundred years before the Omàmiwinini would again have a village there. Then, when that happened, the island and the village would be under the protection of over four hundred of the best Algonquin warriors in the Nation, under the leadership of one of his great grandchildren, Tessouat.

Now I was travelling with the greatest force of warriors ever gathered in the history of the Allied Nations, for an attack to the south on the Haudenosaunee. My world had been turned upside down, and I had been given no time to grieve. My anguish was contained to my heart, mind, and soul, with revenge the only answer that could possibly soothe the pain of the tremendous loss of my family members. The loss of my wife and brother was devastating. I felt like I was going to be physically sick. This was a heart scar that would never heal.

Panther Scar, his warriors, and captives had been on the river for four days, and they were starting to think about the comforts of their village. Their people had always been under the thumb of the stronger Omàmiwinini to the north. In the past few years, some of the tribes that had always been at war with each other were now starting to realize that it would be to their advantage to form alliances to stand strong against these northern enemies. The Ouendat and their allies, the Nippissing, Innu, Malecite, and Algonquin, were a formidable force. Since this loose confederacy had formed, there were now enough warriors to raid north of the big lake and inflict casualties on the foes of the Haudenosaunee.

Panther Scar's people were a powerful military force and every young man's duty was to train as a warrior. The Haudenosaunee were continually at war with one or more of their enemies and at times among themselves.

Panther Scar was from the Wolf Clan (Okwàho). Under Haudenosaunee law, clan mothers chose candidates as their chiefs. The women controlled ownership of the homes and had a veto power over council decisions. The position of the Clan Mothers was hereditary. As a chief appointed by a Clan Mother, Panther Scar answered to her and only she and death could take his chief's antlers away.

The Ouendat, Nippissing, and Omàmiwinini to the north were fierce warriors and always had been dangerous enemies. On the north side of the big lake there was a huge buffer zone between the Haudenosaunee and these Nations. All Natives hunted in these lands, but none took up residence here. No one would risk living in this area because of the close proximity to each other. Only death and destruction would be the outcome of that endeavour.

Ten years ago Panther Scar and three of his friends decided they would earn their place around the council fire by raiding to the north in the land of the Omàmiwinini. Their plan was to ambush a small band out fishing or a lone hunter or two. However, what started out to be a quick hit and run by Panther Scar and his friends turned out to be a nightmare.

Panther Scar had heard stories of shapeshifters from his elders but had never seen or experienced one first hand until that day ten springs ago.

Panther Scar and his three companions had been following a small stream that was teeming with suckers. Lingering behind the others by twenty or so feet, because he had stopped to relieve himself, the group had come about a stretch of the stream where they saw a lone man fishing on the opposite bank. Without any thought, the first man, Grouse Feather, charged through the water to make the kill. What followed was like a fast moving storm, everything happened so fast. Grouse Feather dropped halfway across the stream with a spear protruding through the back of his neck. Little Bird and He Who Walks Tall reached the bank at the same time. Here a black monster of a cat tore Little Bird to shreds. At the same time, furious club blows were pummelling the other friend, He Who Walks Tall by a lame youth with battle skills unlike anything Panther Scar had ever seen. When his companions had started their attack, he had still been trying to catch up. He had made the stream with water up to his knees and the black monster of a cat charging him. As the cat ran toward him, the river, the birds singing, all seemed to be in slow motion. He thought, "Is this what it is like before death?" He watched as the animal bounded through the stream at him. Every time that the beast hit the river, water splashed over its heavily muscled body. He dropped his club and fumbled for an arrow but the demon was upon him, and with one swipe of its enormous paw the animal tore the skin from his face and shoulder. At first, there was no pain, only shock. Then Mitigomij called off the cat and told Panther Scar to leave with his life. The enemy warrior just stood there listening to the cat scream, all the time watching the blood of him and his friends wash around his legs.

The cat turned and walked away with the lame one and they disappeared into the woods. As far as he was concerned that day, he had encountered Michabo the trickster god and the inventor of fishing. The creature had to be Gichi-Anami'e-bizhiw. No other explanation would ever convince him otherwise at that moment in time. Standing there, the shock started to wear off, followed by sudden and intense pain. He knew that he had to find a beehive to treat his wounds or the infection and loss of blood would kill him.

It took many days for him to make it back to his village in a near death state. The Shaman saved Panther Scar's life once he arrived home, but there would be hideous physical scars. Once he was well enough to tell his story, the council and his father believed him to be a coward. They questioned him as to why he lived and his friends died. He had to have run. An enemy would never grant their foe life. Panther Scar was lying according to the chiefs. They banished him until he could prove he deserved to be a Haudenosaunee warrior.

For the next ten years he raided to the south against their enemies, doing it on his own to try to regain the trust of his father and the council. Many enemy warriors had met their death on these forays.

Finally, after many years, younger warriors started to join with him on the warpath. Corn Dog was one of the first. It became a known fact that if young warriors wanted to prove themselves that they could follow the scarred one.

Panther Scar became indebted to Corn Dog. This great friend hunted and raided with him and proved to the other young men that Panther Scar was not a coward or bad luck. Soon the two of them had over twenty warriors at their disposal.

Then something happened that changed the thinking of the Clan Mothers and council. His people captured a couple of Algonquin warriors who told them that Panther Scar's adversary that fateful day had been Mitigomij and his panther Makadewà Wàban. They also told Panther Scar's people that Mitigomij spared his life that day. Now his people realized that it was not cowardice that had saved his life. Nevertheless, Panther Scar still believed that this entity and his animal were shapeshifters.

His men had slain many Algonquins on this war trail, but again the Shapeshifter had eluded him, killing exceptional warriors in the process. Panther Scar owed this demon his life, but he still wanted to slay him, for the pain, disfigurement, and the shunning of his people toward him. He was now a warrior who gave no quarter and killed his enemies with a euphoric pleasure. He often wondered that when his time came, would there be pain or would it be a sudden exhilarated release from what he had become?

It would only be a couple of days until Panther Scar reached the big rapids, then another day to the river (Richelieu) that would take them to the safety of their home. The captives had resigned themselves to their destinies and were no longer wailing and calling for their sons and husbands. The young boys captured would become Haudenosaunee warriors, replacing the men who had died in this battle. They had raided with over one hundred and twenty warriors, but had lost eleven men in the battle and twice as many had suffered wounds. With Corn Dog and his men away, Panther Scar was down to less than sixty-five able-bodied warriors to propel the boats and to look after the wounded and captives.

The sky was crystal blue. The sun was shining brightly, reflecting off the river and causing everyone in the boats to glow with the sweat and the water that they tossed on their bodies to keep cool. The only sounds heard were the paddles in the water and a pair of màng (loons) calling out to each other.

As soon as they landed at the portage, Panther Scar instructed several of his men to obtain some fish and waterfowl. Others he sent into the forest to hunt for game. After setting up guards around the camp, three warriors travelled back up the river to see if anyone was following. Panther Scar was still worried about the lack of warriors in the village they had attacked; there should have been another twenty or thirty. If he were right in his concern, they would be relentless in pursuit, unless Corn Dog came upon them and alleviated the problem. His friend Corn Dog was brash, trustworthy, and always wanting to prove himself a great friend and warrior.

Mitigomij and the twins kept pace with me, Miskwì, and Kinòz-i Inini. The wolf and small dog lay in the bottom of the canoe sound asleep. In the twins' boat, the big cat sat and watched like a vigilant sentry. Nothing escaped this animal's sight or senses. He was like the early morning mist — eerie, secretive, and dangerous. Like the mist, that has only one master, the sun, Makadewà Wàban only answered to Mitigomij. The panther would kill in defence of my brother without hesitation, but small children could pull on his tail and ears at will when on the rare occasion he would come into the village.

The weather was being good to us as we started our voyage. Everyone on the river with us knew what lay ahead, and that we had to make quick time. The food that we brought would have to last the way, as there was no time for hunting. With no women and children to fish from the boats, the men dropped a fishing line and took their chances on catching something. Much to our surprise, Nokomis supplied us with enough fish to make good stews every night. Time was of the essence and everyone knew that we had to catch an enemy that had a substantial head start. In all probability, it would end at their village.

What we had planned in the Ouendat Nation to be a two-pronged attack had developed into a revenge and rescue mission.

My heart was still heavy from my loss, and I had a bitter taste in my mouth. My stomach was queasy and my mind reeled from what had happened. A strong and vibrant community now laid burnt and destroyed, most of my relatives and friends all dead or captured. The fire had prevented the Nation from gathering for the summer, and in turn weakened the Omàmiwinini. The Haudenosaunee had sensed this weakness and acted with a swift and decisive strike. When Mother Nokomis made the decision that my people were included with her plants and animals in this fire renewal, Kitchi Manitou could not protect us. Our lives seemed to be a never-ending cycle of survival against all the elements that Cluskap sent against us.

The original plans that had been made in the Ouendat village was to arrive at my village, feast, hunt, and wait for the Nippissing and more of my Nation. During this time, we would acquire a store of food and make our weapons for the planned raid. However, the raid of the Haudenosaunee threw these plans to the wind. Though we had many warriors on this foray, we had planned on more, and we had a low supply of food and continually were working on making weapons during our nightly camps. The main makeup of our force was Ouendat and Nippissing, with hopefully a strong contingent of Omàmiwinini led by Pangì Shìshìb coming behind us.

When Panther Scar's scouts returned, they told him that they had travelled up the river a long way and had not seen any enemy action.

"Thank you. Have something to eat, our hunters were successful," he replied.

We had made good time in the two days we had been on the Kitcisìpi. Mitigomij never fell off the pace. He was an excellent canoeist, and the warriors who were his aides moved him quickly through the portages on the litter. With no women and children along, everyone had jobs to do when making camp for the evening, such as gathering firewood, erecting cedar lean-tos, and cooking. The Ouendat warriors were young and eager, always taking responsibility for posting night guards.

The third day started out very hot and humid. By mid-afternoon, the temperature rapidly dropped and the sky turned black, shutting out the sun, turning day into night. The wind came up so strong that it started to turn our boats. A sudden bolt of lightning struck so close that our boat could feel the heat and our hair stood up from the force. The sound was deafening and we were momentarily dazed. Our heads rang from the percussion. Looking around behind us, we saw that a canoe with Ouendat men had taken the full force of the blast. Their canoe was on fire and two of the warriors were floating face down in the water. The third man sat in the boat screaming in pain from the fire that was engulfing him. The boat then sank, taking the writhing warrior to a watery grave and in turn soothing his pain.

Then the rain came with such a force that it threatened to swamp our boats if we did not make it to shore. Struggling to keep the winds and the rain from capsizing us, we frantically headed to land. All around us vessels were turning over and warriors were throwing ropes to the men in the water to help them to shore. Once onto shore we dragged the boats into the forest, tipped them, and crawled under for shelter.

Everyone was sodden from the rain, making it a very uncomfortable day waiting out the storm. The rain kept on until just before nightfall. Then we all emerged from our birch bark shelters and hastily started fires. Once the men got fires going, we built them as large as we could, using the light to repair our canoes.

Ojàwashkwà Animosh, Ozàwà Onik, and I then met to make plans after we were sure the camp was organized.

"All my people survived," I said. "Ozàwà Onik, I'm deeply sorry for the loss of your three warriors by the lightning strike."

"Thank you for your sorrow. They were three young men on their first war trail. Their families will mourn them for they were good providers and carried many promises as warriors."

Ojàwashkwà Animosh then said, "I lost two men when the boats started to capsize. In all the confusion, they disappeared into the water and were swept downstream. If we find their bodies I want to bury them."

Ozàwà Onik and I agreed to Ojàwashkwà Animosh's request.

We had lost valuable time and had no way of knowing if our quarry had suffered the same setback from the storm.

The runners who had left the village were our fastest, and we anticipated that they would meet up with a Malecite or Innu hunting party. We needed a diversion at the rapids if there was any hope of slowing the Haudenosaunee down.

Panther Scar had taken his time going downriver, even though all the time thinking that we were only a small force of thirty or forty pursuers behind them. The storm had caught them at a portage, and they sheltered themselves in relative comfort. He had wanted his friend Corn Dog to catch up before they reached the big rapids near where the two big rivers and large island converged on each other. They would reach this area in the next day or so, and there they could only wait for a maximum of two days for Corn Dog.

When they reached the rapids Panther Scar's force would only be two or three days from home. Little did Panther Scar know that a huge force was a day and a half behind and that there were also enemies coming down the river from the east. His men were well fed and rested; he had not pushed them hard at all on the river. The women and children captives fished from their boats with the understanding that if they were unsuccessful they would not be eating. At night they tied the women up and the young ones remained free. They would not go anywhere without their mothers or aunts.

29

RETRIBUTION

OJÀWASHKWÀ ANIMOSH, OZÀWÀ ONIK, and I had been sending scouts out ahead of the main force every day. We did not want to stumble onto a Haudenosaunee ambush.

An ambush was a sign of clever fighting. To kill from a trap was a better-thought-out strategy than a frontal attack. A well-laid trap always had an enhanced success rate because of the advantage of surprise and the opportunity to kill and disable the enemy without significant losses on your side. Anterior attacks that resulted in hand-to-hand battles never ended well for either side; casualties were always high for both sides. Those who killed from safety always showed superior strength and to be merciful was a sign of weakness, unless it was to make a point to the enemy. An enemy who you let live would always come back with revenge in his heart.

At the end of the fourth day, I called my small force of fifteen Omàmiwinini warriors together.

"My fellow warriors, when the battle starts I want all of you to be with me. I hope that Pangì Shìshìb and Minowez-I will eventually catch up, but for now, this is all we have to represent our Nation. I want us to fight together as one unit among the Ouendat, Nippissing, and whoever else joins us from the east. If I am to die in the future it has to be among Omàmiwinini warriors."

I then turned to the four young warriors who were responsible for Mitigomij and said, "If the enemy escapes from us at the rapids we will have to chase them to the south into their lands. Mitigomij will not be left behind; you have a great responsibility to help him keep up to us. We need the fighting abilities of him and the black one. He is great medicine and Kitchi Manitou has always smiled upon Mitigomij."

"Mahingan, Mitigomij will keep up. You have our word," replied my nephew Wàbek.

On their last portage, they had seen where their enemy had camped. The signs showed they were only a day ahead. They would reach the rapids in the next day or so and then the final battle would start.

Kàg had travelled this way a long time ago when he was a young warrior. They had raided a summer fishing camp of Haudenosaunee east of the rapids, and he had captured a beautiful woman he called Kinebigokesì. She became his wife and bore him the twin sons who now travelled with him as warriors. Now, after all these years, her own people had recaptured her, and by now they have probably come to realize that she was one of them. If this had happened, they would return her to her family unharmed.

Kàg had told his sons who their mother was and that the enemy would not harm her. This calmed their fears, but they still had other relatives with the enemy and their fate would depend on many things. One was that if our war party pressed them too hard they would start killing the captives who slowed them down.

The pursuers paddled through the next day and that night. When they camped they prepared themselves for the oncoming battle. Everyone filled their food pouches full of Ouendat corn and whatever dried meat that they could find. If during a battle a warrior separated from his people, he would then have to survive on what he carried to evade capture or death at the hands of his foe. That night we danced and drummed to ask our ancestors and Kitchi Manitou for guidance and protection. The next morning we adorned ourselves with paint to put fear into our enemies and to give us courage.

When we reached the rapids at noon the next day we knew we were closing in. The cooking fires we found were from the previous day. The Haudenosaunee would now travel east toward the river (present-day Richelieu River) that would take them to their homeland. Here would be the chance we would need to catch them. If the Innu and the Malecite had answered our call and come down the big river from the east, they could intercept them before they reached the waterway to their homelands.

❄ ❄ ❄

Panther Scar's men were nearing the last leg for home. They were hugging the shoreline, staying in the small bays and avoiding the open water. This kept them from detection if there were any of their enemies in the vicinity. If discovered, they could quickly reach shore and the cover of the forest.

It was now past noon that day, and they had been making good time away from the rapids. They had lingered close to two days waiting for Corn Dog to show; by then the risk was too high to remain any longer. Corn Dog would have to catch up with his group when he could. Panther Scar thought that his friend might have come across the small band of warriors that he was sure were trailing them.

"Panther Scar," a voice from one of his scouts woke him from his thoughts.

"Yes," he replied.

"Just before the entrance of the river we are travelling to, we sighted over twenty boats with just warriors and a few women. They are mostly Innu and a few Malecite."

"How close are they to us?" asked the Haudenosaunee chief.

"They are on the opposite side of the river and travelling fast!" replied the scout.

Panther Scar had his warriors hurry to shore, pulling the boats up and hiding them. The captives were then bound, gagged, and placed under guard. He would not risk a battle here. The enemy numbers were close to his, and he would suffer losses that would greatly hinder their chances of getting home safely.

From the cover of the thick forest, Panther Scar and his warriors had waited for the enemy's boats to pass. After a half hour the canoes came into sight. He could make out a few Algonquin and Malecite warriors, but the main body was Innu. He counted sixty-two warriors and five women in nineteen boats. He did not think they were a hunting party as there were too many. Seeing the Algonquins made him suspect that these men were somehow tied in with the village that he and his men had destroyed. Noticing also that they had no advance scouts and the urgency that they were paddling made him think that they were travelling to meet someone. Now he was sure he had made the right decision to hide.

The Haudenosaunee waited in the forest for a half hour or so to make sure the enemy had long gone. It had been very hard to stay still for the hour they were in the thick stand of pine, cedar and underbrush. The biting insects were feasting on their bare skin. Because the captives had all their limbs tied, they were in intense agony from the biting, with their faces and bodies starting to swell from the stings. They had run out of goldenseal mixture to repel their swarms and had to put the smudges out when they entered into hiding in the forest. Once back on the river they relit the fungi smudges and alleviated the hordes of bugs that had trailed them out of the woods.

Panther Scar now knew that this escape had become a race against time. He would have to make the river that would take them south and then after a day and a half enter the forest for the final leg home. Speed was of the essence now; any faltering on their part could mean an all out battle with our oncoming force. He told his warriors that once they landed again on shore, to kill any captives that could not keep up.

Meanwhile, behind the Haudenosaunee the Algonquins and our allies portaged around the rapids and struck out to the east on the river. We had not gone far when we joined the Innu, Malecite, and our runners, who days before had left our village to find these allies. They told us that they had not come across the Haudenosaunee. We knew that they were not far ahead of us, and that they could not have reached the southbound river before the Innu group had travelled past there. That meant they had seen our allies coming upriver and had been able to hide while they passed. We were close and they knew it. We made the decision to double time our paddle strokes until nightfall; we had to catch them before they went ashore and headed into the forest and to their hunting trail home. We would be at a disadvantage once they reached the forest and were able to lay a Haudenosaunee ambush.

Our war party now numbered over three hundred warriors. There still was no sign of Pangì Shìshìb and Minowez-I, who could add another one hundred warriors to the group.

That night we camped about a half-day's travel west of the river. The chiefs made a decision to send a dozen men ahead to try to find the enemy. We would find out tomorrow how close we were to them.

First dawn found all the boats in the water striving for the Haudenosaunee southern escape route with hope that this would be the day that we could wreak revenge on them.

Toward midday, the lead canoes yelled back that the scouts were in sight and travelling in haste toward us.

The scouts who had been Ouendat and Innu reached the boat of Ozàwà Onik and relayed the news to him.

Ozàwà Onik turned and said, "The scouts have sighted our adversaries, and they are only a short distance ahead. We are very close to the northern flowing river of the Haudenosaunee. My men tell me that the enemy has already reached there and are heading down it as I speak. We all know that they will have to portage past the rapids and the waterfall. This is where we have to catch them before they make their break to the forest down river from the falls."

In no time at all, the massive cavalcade of canoes and warriors headed for the Haudenosaunee River. We reached the mouth of the river and sped toward the falls and the battle that we knew would happen there. If our enemy escaped from us there, the chase would become dangerous, with us having to pursue them into their homeland. The fall season was coming on and we could find ourselves caught in an early snow.

"Panther Scar, we have just come from our back trail and we are being followed by an immense force," said Long

Arm, one of his scouts. "We are outnumbered at least five to one and they will be upon us in less than an hour. The main parts of the force are dogs of the Ouendat Nation. We have fought them many times, and they are relentless."

Panther Scar replied, "They have caught us here at the portage and we cannot make it above the falls before they get here. Hurry to the front and tell the first boat through that they have to go now. They will have to travel as fast as they can to our nearest village, bringing back as many warriors as they can to hold off this force from entering our lands."

Panther Scar then turned to his remaining sixty or so warriors. He told them to take the captives and tie them to trees near the end of the portage.

He needed ten men to come with him; they had less than an hour to set some traps to slow the enemy down once they hit the shore. The rest of his men were to prepare an ambush to repel over three hundred of us. He hoped beyond hope that the lame one was with them, and if he were, he would get his retribution.

I kept my warriors close. With the addition of the three runners who had found and persuaded the Innu and Malecite to come to our aid, I now had eighteen in my small force along with a dog, wolf, and a hell cat. They would make their mark on the enemy. I had no doubt about this.

The canoes landed on the portage shore with no resistance. The men disembarked in droves, with my small band of warriors and me in the middle.

Then without warning men started screaming and dropped to the ground in agony with blood coming out of their feet and their hands as they tried to stop themselves falling to the ground. The Haudenosaunee had buried small wooden stakes in the earth with just the points sticking out and also had laid thorns among the forest cover of leaves. This ruse had been designed to slow us down, and it worked very well. Over twenty warriors had stepped on the stakes and then fallen into the thorns. It would now slow the whole force down looking for the remainder of the traps on the trail. This wasted time would help our rivals set their ambush. They knew they were outnumbered, but they were not going to die easily.

After what seemed an eternity, the ground was cleared and we continued our march toward the falls. The portage was half a league long and took about two hours to travel with boats and supplies. We had neither, but were slowed down by the uncertainty of what lay ahead.

After travelling for about half an hour, the enemy struck. Arrows rained down upon us from the woods. They struck down many of the men before they could raise their skin and wooden shields up for protection. During the initial onslaught, my small force lost three warriors to wounds. Two of the runners had been hit, plus Nijamik. All had been struck in the upper bodies with arrows.

Because of the slow travel, Mitigomij had been able to keep up. I turned to look at him from our hiding place and observed as he slung his slingshot high into a pine tree. The result of this action was watching a man tumbling down through the tree snapping branches as he fell with a resounding thump to the ground.

Ozàwà Onik and Ojàwashkwà Animosh gathered all of the men who had large wooden shields and faced them forward. Then the rest of us with the smaller skin shields gathered in the middle with them over our heads. With a blood-curdling Ouendat scream, Ojàwashkwà Animosh led us to battle into the woods. The dog and wolf were at my feet as we charged. Arrows rained down again and some men dropped from the formation as they were struck through openings in our moving fortress. We reached the thick pine woods with a crash. The enemy had pared our force down by about sixty dead and wounded from the time we had come ashore, but now it was hand-to-hand combat.

The first man I crashed into drove his war club into my shield with such force that he knocked it out of my hand. He then caught my right arm with a knife slash that sliced my skin open three or four inches. Swinging my club I caught him a glancing blow off his shoulder, knocking him to one knee, where he proceeded to catch me on the left shin with his club, knocking me to the ground where I thought I would meet my death. I rolled away just in time to see the small dog and Ishkodewan lunge at the man and tear chunks of skin from his body as he screamed in pain and tried to crawl away from the pair.

Now the whole battle seemed surreal as I lay there with my two animals guarding me. I was in immense pain from the knife wound and my badly gashed leg.

I watched as the two warrior women Agwanìwon Ikwe and Kìnà Odenan along with Kànikwe hacked two Haudenosaunee to death with their knives and clubs. The two twins fought side by side with their father Kàg and uncle Mònz. They were battling through the enemy trying to reach their mother who was tied to a tree.

However, the strangest thing I saw was an Innu man with what I thought was an enormous knife. He killed one enemy warrior by cutting his head off with a two handed swing of the weapon. Then, swinging the weapon again, he cut a man's arm off.

Lying propped up on my good arm, I watched as the Haudenosaunee were slowly dying from our over-powering force. Then, turning my head toward the screaming of Mitigomij's panther, I watched as the final death dance took place.

Makadewà Wàban had two men cornered against a large boulder. One man lunged at him with a spear, but the big cat effortlessly jumped over the weapon and came down on the man with bone-crushing fury. The screams of the man and cat caught the attention of all who were fighting, bringing the battle to a standstill. Makadewà then turned and faced the other Haudenosaunee, but Mitigomij called him off. The man turned to look at my brother, and I could see the scars. This was the great chief of the Haudenosaunee, Panther Scar.

Mitigomij said, "It is I who you want. We have unfinished business, Panther Scar. I should have killed you all those years ago!"

"My people say you and that cat are shapeshifters, but today I will kill you before all your people and allies showing them you bleed the blood of a man, and that you are not a creature of the gods," said Panther Scar.

Now all eyes were turned toward these two adversarial warriors.

It was at that moment I arose and proceeded toward the two warriors.

"Panther Scar, it is I who you fight today!"

"And what or who are you?" he replied.

"I am Algonquin! My brother spared your life once; therefore he has not the right to go back on that gesture and slay you here today. It is I who will take his place in this struggle. You will die at my hand. You know what I am. Now, who I am is Mahingan, brother of Mitigomij, leader of the Omàmiwinini." I then turned toward my brother. "Mitigomij, today you have to grant me the grace to fight this battle."

"Mahingan, I am proud to relent in your stead," he replied.

"It does not matter to me who I kill first," interjected Panther Scar. "Because, Mahingan, after I have delivered my death strike to you, I will slay your brother!"

Panther Scar rushed me with his war club in his right hand held high and his knife in his left.

I was seeping blood from my wounds and my left leg was almost numb from the pain. I dropped on my good knee just as Panther Scar swung his weapon. The war club made a swooshing sound as it narrowly missed my head. I drove my knife into his left thigh as he lunged past me. His screams from the sudden pain echoed through the forest. Turning, he lashed out at me with his knife and gashed a chunk of skin from my left shoulder.

Turning aside the pain in my body I gripped my war club with two hands and swung with all my might at the back of his legs. I could hear bone break upon contact. As he dropped to the ground, I rose to my feet and bludgeoned him until he quit moving. At that moment there was a sudden stillness on the battlefield and forest. Not a sound was heard except for crows' echoing calls from over the river. I turned and looked at Mitigomij and he nodded his head in my direction.

Not a word was said from all who watched. It was stone silence until a Malecite warrior ran up the trail shouting that there was more of the enemy coming up the river above the falls.

Mitigomij turned to him and said, "Take this Panther Scar's head and put it on a spear. Carry it to the river along with any prisoners. Hold the spear up so the ones who come up the river can set eyes on who it is. Then kill the captives and shove them into the river for them to see. They will turn back because they will then realize that only death will greet them here."

With those words from my brother, the head of Panther Scar was skewed on a spear and taken along with the captives to the river.

As I stood there looking over the field of slaughter, I wondered what the future held for me. My wounds would heal. I had a son to raise and still two brothers to hunt and fight beside, but our village was destroyed.

Then, as I was still pondering my days ahead, the Innu with the large knife walked by.

Stopping him, I asked, "What is your name?

"Makadewà Nigig (Black Otter)," he replied.

"What is that weapon?" I asked.

"It is called an ajaweshk (sword)," said Makadewà Nigig.

"Who made it for you?"

"No one. I won it in battle."

"What Native warrior carried that?" I asked.

"It was not a Native. The man I took this from had hair the color of the kìzis (sun) and skin the color of the wìgwàs mitig (birch tree). He was covered in furs and wore a hat as hard as a rock with horns in it. He came in a big boat with many paddles and many men. They tried to take our women as they were fishing along the big river shore. Our men attacked and drove them off, but not before many died on both sides. These men fought with great skill. The man I had slain killed at least three of my brethren with this weapon before I shot him with an arrow. He was a great warrior and this weapon has powerful magic."

Makadewà Nigig then said, "When you get better, Mahingan, maybe one day we will fight these strange men side by side."

"Makadewà Nigig, where did these strangers come from?"

Without a word Makadewà Nigig disappeared into the forest.

"Mahingan, Mahingan!" It was Kàg. "When we rescued my wife Kinebigokesì a group of the Haudenosaunee escaped with some captives. We followed them as they ran to the river. They quickly were rescued by the group that had come up river. As they were loading the captives in the canoes I was shocked to see one of them was Wàbananang! Mahingan, your wife, she is alive!"

GLOSSARY

For an Algonquin talking dictionary, please go to *www. hilaroad.com/camp/nation/speak.htm.*

Adjidamò	Squirrel
Àgimag	Snowshoes
Agwanìwon Ikwe	Shawl woman
Agwingos	Chipmunk
Ajaweshk	Sword
Ajowà Okiwan	Blunt nose
Akandò	Ambush
Amik	Beaver
Amik Pìwey	Beaver fur
Amik-wìsh	Beaver lodge
Amikwànò	Beaver tail
Andeg	Crow

Àndjig-o	Pregnant
Anìb	Elm
Anìdjànìl	Doe
Animosh	Dog
Anit	Spear
Anokì	Hunt
Asin	Stone
Asinwàbidì	Stone elk
Askootasquash	Squash
Ayàbe Mònz	Bull moose
Ayàbe Tibik-kìzis	Buck Moon / July
Azàhan	Beans
Chìmàn	Canoe
Cluskap	The creator force
Epangishimodj	West
Esiban	Raccoon
Gichi-Anam'e-bizhow	The Fabulous Night Panther
Haudenosaunee	Iroquois
Hochelagans	A tribe from the island near the rapids of the big river
Ininàtig Nòpimìng	Maple forest
Innu	Montagnais
Ishkodewan	Blaze
Kabun	God of the west wind
Kàg	Porcupine
Kàgàgi	Ravens
Kaibonokka	God of the north wind
Kàkàskanedjìsì	Nightingale
Kànikwe	No hair
Kigàdjigwesì	Hunter

Kìgònz	Fish
Kìjekwe	Honoured woman
Kìjik Anìbìsh	Cedar tea
Kìnà Odenan	Sharp tongue
Kinebigokesì	Cricket
Kinebik	Snakes
Kiniw	Eagle
Kinònjepìriniwak	People of the Pickerel Waters below Allumette Island
Kinòz-i Inini	Tall Man
Kìshkijigewin Tibik-kìzis	Harvest Moon / September
Kitchi Manitou	Father of Life
Kitcisìpiriniwak	People of the Great River
Kìzis	Sun
Kòkòkòhò	Owl
Kwìngwayàge	Wolverine
Kwingwishì	Gray jay
Mahingan	Wolf
Makadewà Kìkig	Black sky
Makadewà Nigig	Black otter
Makadewà Wàban	Black dawn
Makòns	Bear cub
Makwa	Bear
Mànabìsì	Swan
Mandàman	Corn
Mandàmin Animosh	Corn dog
Màng	Loon
Manòmin	Rice
Mashkodesì	Quail

Matàwackariniwak	People of the Bulrush shore along the Madawaski River
Michabo	The Great Hare Trickster God
Mìgàdinàn-àndeg	War crow
Mìgàdinàn Pagamàgin	War club
Mìgàdinàn Wàgàkwad	War axe
Mìkisesimik	Wampum belt
Mikkwì	Blood
Minisìnò	Warrior
Minòkami Màwndwewehinge	Late spring call together
Minowez-I	War dance
Mishi-Pijiw	Panther
Mishi-Pijiw Odjìshiziwin	Panther scar
Misise	Turkey
Miskominag Anìbìsh	Raspberry leaf tea
Miskoz-i Animosh	Red Dog
Miskoz-i Kekek	Red Hawk
Mitigomij	Red oak
Mitigwàbàk	Hickory
Mòkomàn	Knife
Mònz	Moose
Mònzwegin	Moose hide
Nàbe	Buck
Nàme	Sturgeon
Namebin	Sucker fish
Nanapàdjinikesì	Mice
Nasemà	Tobacco

Nìbachi	Near Muskrat Lake
Nìbawiwin	Marriage
Nigig	Otter
Nìjamik	Two Beaver
Nika	Geese
Nòjek	Female bear
Nokomis	Earth Mother
Nòpimìng	Forest
Odàbànàk	Toboggan
Odey	Heart
Odeyimin Tibik-kìzis	Strawberry Moon / June
Odjìg	Fisher
Ogà	Pickerel
Ogìshkimansì	Kingfisher
Ojàwashkwà Anismosh	Blue dog
Okanisì	Grosbeak
Okwàho	Wolf clan
Omàmiwinini	Algqonquin
Onàbanad Tibik-kìzis	Crust Moon / March
Onigam	Portage
Onimikì	Thunder
Onzibàn	Sap
Ouendat	Huron
Ozàwà Onik	Yellow arm
Ozàwàbik	Copper
Pàgàdowewin	Lacrosse
Pagamàgin Ozid	Clubfoot
Pagidjiwanàn	Resting place on a portage
Pangì Shìshìb	Little duck
Pashkwadjàsh	Coyote

Pijakì	Buffalo
Pijiw	Lynx
Pikodjisi	Blackfly
Pikwàkogwewesì	Blue jay
Pimidàbàjigan	Travois
Pineshìnjish	Birds
Pìsà Animosh	Small dog
Pìtòshkob	Pond
Piwàkwad	Ball
Sàgaiganininiwak	People of the Lake
Sagime	Mosquito
See-Bee-Pee-Nay-Sheese	River bird
Shawano	God of the south wind
Shàwanong	South
Shigàg	Skunk
Shìshìb	Duck
Shìwanìbìsh	Dandelion
Sìbì	River
Wàbananang	Morning star
Wàbàndagawe Animosh	White dog
Wàbanong	East
Wabidì	Elk
Wàbigon Tìbik-kìzis	Flower Moon / May
Wàbòz	Rabbit
Wabun	God of the east wind
Wàgàkwad	War axe
Wàginogàns	Lodges
Wàgosh	Fox
Wajashk	Muskrat

Wajashk Sàgahigan and Sìbì	Muskrat Lake and River
Wàwàsamòg	Lightning
Wàwàshekshi	Deer
Wàwìyeyano	Full moon
Weski-nibawidjig	Newlyweds
Wewebasinàbàn	Slingshot
Weynusse	Turkey buzzard
Wìbwàte	Corridor
Wìdigemàgan	Wife
Wìgwàs-chimàn	Birch bark canoes
Wìgwàs mitig	Birch tree
Wìskwey	Sinew
Wìyagiminan Tibik-kìzis	Fruit Moon / August
Wìyàs	Meat
Wysoccan	Intoxicating poison
Zigosis	Mother-in-law

ALGONQUIN PRONUNCIATION GUIDE

From *www.native-languages.org/algonquin.*

VOWELS

Character:	How To Say It:
a	Like the *a* in *what*.
à	Like the *a* in *father*.
e	Like the *a* in *gate* or the *e* in *red*.
è	Like *a* in *pay*.
i	Like the *i* in *pit*.
ì	Like the *ee* in *seed*.
o	Like the *u* in *put*.
ò	Like the *o* in *lone*.

DIPHTHONGS

Character:	How To Say It:
aw	Like *ow* in *cow*.
ay	Like *eye*.
ew	This sound doesn't really exist in English. It sounds a little like saying the "AO" from "AOL" quickly.
ey	Like the *ay* in *hay*.
iw	Like a child saying *ew!*
ow	Like the *ow* in *show*.

CONSONANTS

Character:	How To Say It:
dj	Like *j* in *jar*.
k	Like *k* in *key* or *ski* (see Soft Consonants, below.).
p	Like *p* in *pin* or *spin* (see Soft Consonants, below.)

SOFT CONSONANTS

The Algonquin pronunciation of the consonants *p*, *t*, and *k* is unaspirated between two vowels or after an *m* or *n*. To English speakers, this makes the consonants sound soft. You can hear unaspirated consonants in English after the letter *s*, such as the *k* in *skate* or the *t* in *stir*. If you put your fingers in front of your mouth as you pronounce *kate* and *skate*, you will see that there is no puff of air as you pronounce the unaspirated *k* in *skate*. Algonquin "soft" consonants are pronounced the same way.

kìjig (day) is pronounced [kʰi:jIg], with a hard *k*, but

anokì kìjig (working day) is pronounced [anoki: ki:jIg], with two soft *k*'s.

NASAL VOWELS

Nasal vowels don't exist in English, but you may be familiar with them from French (or from hearing people speak English with a French accent). They are pronounced just like oral ("regular") vowels, only using your nose as well as your mouth. To English speakers, a nasal vowel often sounds like a vowel with a half-pronounced *n* at the end of it. You can hear examples of nasal vowels at the end of the French words "bon" and "Jean," or in the middle of the word "Français."

In Algonquin pronunciation, vowels automatically become nasal before *nd*, *ng*, *nj*, or *nz*. For example, *kìgònz* is pronounced [ki:gō:z], not [ki:go:nz]. Those nasal vowels are a normal part of a native speaker's accent — like English speakers automatically pronouncing the letter *l* differently at the beginning and end of a word — so they are not written. Unlike in Ojibwe, nasal vowels do not occur anywhere else in a word.

BIBLIOGRAPHY

Access Genealogy. *www.accessgenealogy.com*.

Bonnicksen, Thomas M. *America's Ancient Forests: From the Ice Age to the Age of Discovery*. New York: John Wiley & Sons, Inc. 2000.

Borneman, Walter R. *The French and Indian War*. Toronto: HarperCollins Publishers, 2009.

Champlain, Samuel de. *Algonquians, Hurons and Iroquois: Champlain Explores America, 1603–1616*. Translated by Annie Nettleton Bourne. Edited by Edward Gaylord Bourne. Nova Scotia: Brook House Press, 2000.

Clément, Daniel. *The Algonquins*. Gatineau, Quebec: The Canadian Museum of Civilization, 1996.

Ellis, Eleanor. *Northern Cookbook*. Toronto: McClelland & Stewart, 1999.

Empires Collide: The French and Indian War 1754–63. Edited by Ruth Shepard. Great Britain: Osprey Publishing, Midland House, 2006.

Gidmark, David. *Birch Bark Canoe: Living Among the Algonquins*. Toronto: Firefly Books, 1997.

"The History and Origin of the Five Nations." Compiled by Harry Pettengill, Jr. UCE Historian. *www.upstate-citizens.org/Iroquois-origin.htm*.

Josephy, Alvin M., Jr. *The Patriot Chiefs: A Chronicle of American Indian Leadership*. New York: Viking Press, 1976.

McGregor, Ernest. *The Algonquin Lexicon*. The Authority, 1994.

Moore, Tom. *The Plains of Madness*. St. John's: Tomcod Press, 2001.

Nerburn, Kent. *Neither Wolf nor Dog: On Forgotten Roads with an Indian Elder*. Novato, California: New World Library, 2002.

Ray, Arthur J. *I Have Lived Here Since the World Began: An Illustrated History of Canada's Native People*. Toronto: Lester Publishing Ltd., 1996.

Wright, Ronald. *Stolen Continents: The "New World" Through Indian Eyes*. New York: Houghton Mifflin Company, 1993.

MUSEUMS

The Canadian Museum of Civilization

Huronia Museum (Midland, Ontario)

The Plains of Abraham (Quebec City)

The Rooms Provincial Museum (St. John's, Newfoundland)

Sainte-Marie among the Hurons (Midland, Ontario)

Thunder Bay Museum

OF RELATED INTEREST

Broken Circle
Christopher Dinsdale

9781894917155
$8.95

Angry at missing a week of summer video game entertainment, Jesse, a twelve-year-old boy of European/ Native descent, grudgingly follows through with his deceased father's request that he join his Uncle Matthew and cousin Jason at Six Islands, on Georgian Bay, for a special camping trip. Uncle Matthew explains that Jesse's father wanted Jason's vision quest to be his introduction to their Native culture. During their first night around the camp-fire, it is Jesse who has a vision, and the adventure begins. Not only is he swept back in time four hundred years, but he is transformed into a majestic, white-tailed deer. He must now survive the expert hunting skills of his ancestors while somehow rescuing his people before they are destroyed by warfare.

Jak's Story
Aaron Bell

9781554887101
$10.99

Thirteen-year-old Jak Loren is a typical boy with the usual problems a family with older sisters and younger brothers presents. Never mind the troubles at school — bullies and girls!

When Jak goes to the ravine near his home in Brantford to get away from Steven Burke, a bully who's been tormenting him, he discovers the ravine has a history that's much older than he thought. He meets Grandfather Rock, who shares with him the story of the people who have lived near the ravine for thousands of years. Soon Jak's eyes are opened to a new world of beings and respect.

He learns about First Nations people and how their teachings inhabit the spirits of all living things that surround us even today. The tales of the First Nations help Jak to understand that the gift of life is something to be cherished. And when a construction crew arrives in his neighbourhood and threatens his beloved ravine, Jak knows he has to act to save it.

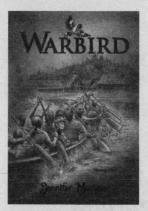

Warbird
Jennifer Maruno

9781926607115
$9.95

In 1647, ten-year-old Etienne yearns for a life of adventure far from his family farm in Quebec. He meets an orphan destined to apprentice among the Jesuits at Fort Sainte-Marie. Making the most impulsive decision of his life, Etienne replaces the orphan and paddles off with the voyageurs into the north country. At Sainte-Marie, Etienne must learn to live a life of piety. Meanwhile, he also makes friends with a Huron youth, Tsiko, who teaches him the ways of his people. When the Iroquois attack and destroy the nearby village, Etienne must put his new skills into practice. Will he survive? Will he ever see his family again?